U0134672

BOOK OF NO SLEEP

無眠詩

點子出版
IDEA PUBLICATION

Preface
推薦序

嗨，正在看這篇序的你，別心急揭開下一頁啊。因為我準備告訴你一個真相——你，正正就是某個恐怖故事中的主角。

不相信？正在偷笑？覺得我胡說八道？其實你只是早就「絕望」得麻木而已。

有説錯嗎？

無止境的學習和應考、為了「生存」所以無法擺脱的工作、每天重複又重複的生活接近毫無意義、甚至被奪去自由和權利……恐怖故事的橋段幾乎每天都在身邊發生。不單只你，還有我和其他人，其實全都是當中的主角。

然而，最恐怖的當然不是以上提及的例子，而是……你已經花了差不多一分鐘時間看這篇明天起床就會忘掉的序……咳咳……很恐怖吧？突然就被人騙走了人生寶貴的時間。

但我可以保證，這本書所收錄的故事絕對不會欺騙你的時間。因為你和我所經歷的恐怖橋段，終歸都只是冰山一角……

有心無默

Preface
推 薦 序

Reddit 討論區的 No Sleep 及 Short Scary Stories 版區，可說是高質驚悚故事的泉源。海外高手臥虎藏龍，無論有否寫恐佈小說的經驗，No Sleep 及 Short Scary Stories 都是極適合創作人每日必到的網站。

由選擇故事翻譯，再與每個海外作者傾洽版權，相信都是繁複的過程，很高興點子出版的團隊完成到困難重重的事，成功把外國人的視野帶到本地的文壇。

向西村上春樹

Preface
推薦序

很多人問「創作故事」的過程包含了甚麼？既然創作有個「創」字，那麼一定離不開「創新」，一個讓人讚嘆的點子、一段峰迴路轉的情節、一股震盪人心的情感。

然而矛盾的是，就算再好的作品難免會有前人的影子，例如史蒂芬•金的《撒冷鎮》和《德古拉伯爵》有不少近似的設定情節；《BJ 單身日記》是《傲慢與偏見》的現代中女版；血腥電影《恐怖旅舍》改編自導演聽過的一則泰國傳說。呃……當然還有近年數之不盡，由日本紅到香港以「平常生活突然入了異度空間 / 怪物來襲」作開頭的作品。

這是因為一個優秀的作者一定是個閱讀狂，對故事有種渴望，不論是書籍、短故、新聞都想看一番。史蒂芬 · 金亦都直言不諱地說：「你沒時間閱讀就不要寫作。」上述兩本小説一套電影堪稱當代經典。這都多得因為三名創作人飽覽故事，再培養出個人風格，才孕育出新的經典。

所以這和本書有甚麼關係？這本短篇故事集收集了眾多外國網絡短故，裡頭蘊含了不少有趣的點子，是個難得的寶庫。希望你們除了讀得過癮外，還細心鑽研一下，希望日後能見到更多屬於香港的經典作品。

恐懼鳥

Preface
推薦序

曾經有不少讀者向我們投訴過點子出版的書籍很恐怖很詭秘，令人很不安。甚至有讀者睇完本出版社的《Deep Web File》後，遠赴淫審處投訴，那位中年男讀者指出該書籍「恐懼得連續兩晚超過 48 小時無法入睡」。

有人看到粗口會打冷震，有人看到色情內容會性興奮；一本書籍要多恐怖，才可以令一個人連續兩晚無法入睡，我不知道。我只知這本《無眠書》足以令一個人看完超過兩日無法入睡的原因太多，或許是恐怖到不敢睡、或許是太吸引好看到不願睡、或許是謎團未解開令你心思思不能入睡⋯⋯

余禮禧

Preface
譯者序

首先非常感謝您閱讀這本《無眠書》，希望您在細味故事的同時，亦能使您有所反思及領悟。

由與外國作者洽商，到翻譯內容，再到書本設計，直到完成印刷，前後只花了四個多月時間，無論對於譯者和出版社來說都是一項非常極速的任務。這本作品可說是幾乎在不眠不休的狀態下譯成，《無眠書》由無眠的譯者譯成，實在是相映成趣。

由於此書是中英對照版本，對譯者來說可算是非常有挑戰性，因為只要有地方譯錯了，馬上就會看得出來，所以在此也很感謝編輯替我「執手尾」，盡量避免錯漏。但無可否認的是，原文即使不完美，也是有著作者的心血和英語獨有的韻味，所以我們還是堅持以中英對照的形式把故事呈獻給大家。

雖然故事設定大多都在外國，不像港式的驚慄小說般有著熟悉的背景，但有好幾個故事都透露著一些曾在歐美地區發生的真實罪案，如果您有看過《Deep Web》系列，也可能會知道人口販賣和拐帶兒童的案件實在是多不勝數，您還敢說這些故事只是「老作」嗎？

就我而言，我覺得閱讀每篇故事也像看了一齣微型恐怖片般，雖然沒有圖像和聲效的衝擊，但只單憑想像，其驚慄效果也不亞於電影。裡面有好幾篇故事都和一些經典驚慄電影有著異曲同工之妙，例如：《抖室 Room》（闡述失蹤人口、禁室培慾、拐帶兒童）、《孤疑 Orphan》（揭露孩子陰險的一面）、《恐懼鬥室 Saw》（陷入身不由己的困境，最終自相殘殺）等等。

有時翻譯故事時，感到頭昏腦脹，覺得上班很痛苦、沒有人生意義的時候，我會回想起故事內容，如果要我無窮無盡地不斷重複著死亡及絕望，我還是選擇上班好了。即使此書沒有正能量，也能使您在負能量中找到哪怕只是半點兒的生存意義。

最後希望各位讀者會喜歡《無眠書》，亦請各位多多指教。

補充：在翻譯這些故事時，常常害得我不敢獨個兒上廁所，被同事和朋友取笑了好一陣子。我只能回應說：「你們看過這些故事就不會再那麼處之泰然了，哼。」

陳婉婷

CONTENTS
目 錄

詭譎童話 Insidious Tales

惱人自白 Vexed Confession

心寒覺悟 Frantic Awakening

末日啟示 The Apocalypse

生存規則 Survival Rules

Insidious Tales
詭 譎 童 話

My Family Never Listens to Me

When I was born, my mother cried for me to never leave her. I didn't understand at the time, but somehow I remember it even though I was so young. I stayed around long enough to be brought home.

At 5 years old, I didn't go to school like my older brother. I cried for a chance to go, but my pleas were unheard. I drew on the walls with crayon in frustration, writing my name, David, over and over until the wall was covered. My mother shut herself in her room and cried. My father yelled at my brother who denied everything, but still got timeout.

At 10 years old, my baby sister arrived, taking even more attention from me. I began throwing expensive vases off the table and if that didn't work I'd slam doors. My father began to get angry. My mother would shield my sister and look to my father for help.

At 15 years old I entered the room only to hear my parents talking about moving. I was a little furious. I didn't want to leave. I began to scream. Everything flew past me and at my parents; DVD's, books, and pictures on the wall. They screamed and ducked into their room with my sister.

家人從來都不聽我講話

我出世的時候，媽媽哭著叫我永遠不要離開她。當時我不明白為何她這樣說，雖然當時我年紀還那麼小，但我記得她這樣說過。我待了一段長時間，媽媽才能帶我回家。

我五歲的時候，我不像哥哥般要上學，我求爸媽讓我上學，但他們不理會我。我沮喪地用蠟筆畫牆，不斷寫著我的名字「David」，直到牆寫滿了我的名字。媽媽把自己關在房間，哭了起來。爸爸對著哥哥大吼大叫，雖然哥哥不承認是他做的，但最後還是被罰了。

我十歲的時候，妹妹出世了，更加沒有人關心我了。我開始把昂貴的花瓶從桌子上丟在地下，如果這樣還是沒有人理我，我就會砰地關門。爸爸開始生氣了，媽媽則保護著妹妹，尋求爸爸的協助。

我十五歲的時候進了房間，只為了聽聽爸媽談論搬家的事。我有點生氣，我不想離開。我開始尖叫，DVD、書本和牆壁上的照片，所有東西飛過我身邊，向爸媽的方向飛去。他們尖叫著，然後和妹妹一起躲在房間裡。

I wandered aimlessly around the house, not sleeping. The sun rose and soon my parents did too, but they had a duffle bag on their shoulders. My sister was in my dad's arms. I followed them to the door, ready to leave with them.

I couldn't. I was trapped here. Alone. Forever.

我漫無目的地在房子裡走著，沒有睡覺。太陽升起，過了一會兒，爸媽也起床了，但他們的肩膀上擱著行李袋，而妹妹就躺在爸爸的懷裡。我跟著他們到了門口，準備跟他們一起離開。

我走不了，我被困在這裡，孤獨一人，直到永遠。

Sally was not Allowed Out after Dark

As children, our mothers allowed us to stay out as long as we wanted to play, unless it got very late. The dark wasn't as much of an issue for us as it was for Sally.

Her mother, Mrs. Bucherman kept an eagle-eye over us, almost always, wherever we went to play, and as the day turned to dusk, she'd come snatch Sally and take her back to the house before darkness fell. Sometimes it was in the middle of games, and Sally was often crying and wailing and screaming as her mom often physically lifted her up and carried her back to the house.

"Everyone else gets to stay." fell on deaf ears.

Once we asked her, in hearing distance of her mother, both of who repeated in a mechanic manner. "If you don't get back to your house before darkness falls, the monsters will get you. Your house is safe, it keeps the monsters out."

Sadly, Mrs.Bucherman passed away in an accident one morning, when she seemingly walked into traffic at a busy intersection.

Sally went to live in foster-care.

On her first day back out playing with us, almost as if a wave

Sally 的宵禁

作為孩子的我們，只要想玩，母親就會准許我們到外面玩耍，除非天色已晚。黃昏對我們來說不是怎麼一回事，但對 Sally 來說就不同了。

她的母親 Bucherman 太太會用銳利的眼神看著我們。我們去玩的時候，只要天空變得昏暗，Bucherman 太太總是會抓走 Sally，把她帶回家。有時更會在我們玩遊戲玩得正高興的時候抓走 Sally，她多數會哭泣、哀號和尖叫，因為她母親經常把她舉起來然後帶回家。

「明明其他人都可以留下來……」但她母親充耳不聞。

如果我們叫她留下，而她母親聽到的話，她就會像 Sally 般機械式地重複著：「如果你在入黑之前沒有回到你的房子，怪物就會來抓你，你的房子是安全的，它會把怪物隔在外面。」

可悲的是，有一天早上，Bucherman 太太在一個繁忙的十字路口遇到意外身亡了。

然後 Sally 就被送了去寄養家庭。

of nostalgia hit her, she went running back to her house before darkness fell.

Previously, we'd never dared to go to Sally's house. But now, we decided to follow her. Her new foster parents, the Smiths were nice people.

The patio door was open. Since we were running after Sally we only assumed she left it open for us, so we entered. On the couch was Mrs.Smith's dismembered head. On the floor was her body.

As one of us began to scream, and the rest joined in unison, we saw Sally slowly stand up straight from her crouched position in the corner where we'd not noticed her before. She was holding part of Mrs.Smith's neck, or whatever was left of it, in her mouth.

And then we remembered Mrs.Bucherman's warning about our houses being safe after dark.

She didn't want to keep the monsters out. She wanted to keep them in.

在她回來跟我們一起玩的第一天，她好像被一陣強烈的懷舊感打擊了般，在入黑之前，她就跑回家了。

以前，我們從來不敢去 Sally 的家，但現在我們決定跟著她。Sally 的寄養父母是 Smith 夫婦，他們都很好人。

庭院門是開著的，因為我們跑在 Sally 後面，我們以為是她為我們開的，所以我們進去了。Smith 太太的頭在沙發上，身體在地上。

隨著我們其中一個人開始尖叫，其他人也一起尖叫著。我們之前沒有注意到 Sally 原來蹲了在角落裡，她緩緩的站起來。她叼著 Smith 太太的脖子，或者甚麼剩餘的東西。

然後我們想起 Bucherman 太太的警告，我們的房子入黑之後也是安全的。

她不是想把怪物隔在外面，她是想讓它留在室內。

Kids Say the Weirdest Things

Allison had earned herself a reputation of telling various fanatical tall-tales. "Jimmy fell off of the tallest building in the world!" or "The librarian has a magical dimensional key" or even "Sarah got swallowed up by a giant turtle at the front of the school!"

Most adults would simply smile and shrug off her nonsensical ramblings. Some would become mildly irritated at having their time wasted and shoo Allie away. Of course a few adults had rationalized that there was always a hidden truth to Allison's words, but in the frenzied mind of a toddler, certain things just became muddled.

For example, Jimmy hadn't truly fallen off of 'the tallest building in the world', he had simply fallen off of the plastic tower at the playground, which to a child may very well have been the tallest building in the world. And of course the librarian didn't actually have a 'magical dimensional key', just a boring old key card and scanner. But Sarah? That one was a head-scratcher.

It wasn't until Sarah didn't show up to school for a week, that the connection was made:

From a distance, and in the mind of an oblivious toddler, a black sedan car looked an awful lot like a giant black turtle.

Author: ***YKGem***

童言無忌

每個人都知道 Allison 喜歡把事情説得誇張又荒誕。例如：「Jimmy 從世界上最高的建築物掉下來了！」或是「圖書管理員有一條魔法鑰匙。」甚至是「Sarah 在學校前面被一隻巨型烏龜吞噬了！」

大部分大人都只會聳聳肩，一笑置之，不會理會她的無稽之談。有些大人則會有點惱怒，覺得 Allison 浪費了他們的時間，所以打發她走。當然還有一些大人會把事情合理化，認為 Allison 的話總是隱藏著真相。

舉個例子，Jimmy 不是真的「從世界上最高的建築物」掉下來，他只是從遊樂場一個塑膠製的塔上跌下來而已，可能對一個小孩子來説也是世界上最高的建築物吧。當然那個圖書管理員也不是真的有「魔法鑰匙」，那只是張老舊的鑰匙卡和掃描器而已。但 Sarah 呢？那真是令人頭痛了。

當 Sarah 整整一個禮拜沒有上課了，大家才發現兩者之間的聯繫：

在一個無知的小孩的心中，一輛黑色的轎車從遠處看起來就像一隻巨大的黑龜一樣可怕。

Chicken Soup

Daddy married a new lady. She's supposed to be my new mommy but I don't like her very much, and ever since she started living here I've been getting sick.

She's very good at pretending to be a good mommy. She gives me fresh soup and warm tea with all the honey I want.

But she's still not mommy. She'll never be mommy.

I cry and cry to daddy for him to send her away but he tells me to hush. He tells me that she is doing her very best. That she cries over my health. I should give her a chance.

And the more she takes care of me, the sicker I get. I get so sick, that I end up in a hospital! The doctors make me better, and send me home after a few days.

And then I get sick all over again.

And it happens again and again and again, until the nurses know me by name. The doctors like to ask my daddy lots of questions about mommy. A strange man in a suit and a nice smile talked to me about her too.

雞湯

爸爸娶了個新老婆，她算是我的新媽媽吧，但我不太喜歡她，而且自從她跟我們一起住之後我就一直生病。

她很擅長扮演一個好媽媽的角色，她會給我熬新鮮的湯，也會弄溫茶給我，讓我放多少蜜糖也可。

但她仍然不是我媽媽，她不會是我媽媽。

我不斷哭求爸爸送她走，但爸爸叫我不要吵。他說「新媽媽」已經盡力做到最好了，她擔心我的身體狀況擔心得哭了，所以我應該給她一個機會。

她照顧我愈多，我就生病得愈嚴重。嚴重得我最後要住醫院！醫生們讓我好過來，幾天後就可以出院回家。

然後我又再次生病了。

我一而再再而三地住院又出院，那些護士都知道我的名字了。那些醫生會問爸爸很多關於「媽媽」的問題。一個穿著西裝、面帶微笑的奇怪男人也跟我說過她的事情。

I'm so happy. Daddy says my fake mommy was going away, and I'll never see her again. He looks so mad, but I know he's not mad at me.

He doesn't know I was the one pouring bleach in the soup she used to give me.

我很開心，因為爸爸說那個假媽媽已經走了，以後都不會再見到她了。爸爸看起來很生氣，但我知道他不是生我的氣。

他不知道把漂白劑倒進湯裡的人就是我。

A Kid Just Walked into My Shop and Told Me His Daddy's Dead

I've never dealt with a lost or abandoned child before. I don't deal well with kids as it is, but a lost one, I was way out of my depth.

It was closing time when he walked in.

"Sorry kid, we're closed," I said putting on my coat.
"My daddy's dead, " he said panting heavily, tears beginning to appear on his cheeks.
"Oh no, what happened?" I said crouching in front of him.

Not knowing how to handle the situation, I put my hands on his shoulders.

"Where is he now?"
"At home."
"Where's home?"
"129 Acre Street."
"I know that well, did you just run from there?"

He nodded.

"Are you sure he's dead?"

He nodded again.

有個小孩走進我的店
跟我說他爸爸死了

我從來沒有遇過小孩走失或被遺棄的情況，而且我本來就不擅跟孩子相處，遇上這樣的孩子，就更應付不來了。

打烊的時候，他走進來了。

「小朋友不好意思喔，我們已經關門了。」我邊說邊穿起外套。
「我爸爸死了……」他氣喘吁吁的，眼淚順著臉頰流下來。
「不是吧……發生甚麼事了？」我蹲在他前面。

我不知道如何應對這個狀況，只好把雙手放在他肩膀上。

「你爸爸在哪？」
「在家。」
「你家在哪裡？」
「英畝街 129 號。」
「好的，我知道了，你剛剛從家裡跑出來嗎？」

他點點頭。

「你確定爸爸死了嗎？」

他又點點頭。

"Okay, let's get you back there now and I'll get help."
He backed away and shook his head, "No, Daddy's dead!"
"It'll all be okay, I promise."

Reluctantly he took my hand as I led him out of the shop.

"Hello, what's your emergency?" the woman on the other end of the line asked.
"Hi, I am with a child, he says his Dad has died."
"Okay, what address?"

We rounded the corner and I saw the flashing lights of the vehicles outside the boy's house.

"Looks like someone else has called already. Sorry for wasting your time."
"Not a problem." the woman said and the line went dead.

When we approached the boy gripped my hand tightly.

"Don't worry son, everything will be okay."

We moved through the paramedics and police interviewing neighbours and approached the front door.

"Is your mum inside?" I asked.

「好吧，那你先回家，我找人來幫忙。」
他邊搖著頭邊退後說：「我不要！爸爸死了！」
「好的，沒事的，我保證。」

他不情願地拉著我的手，我帶他走出店門。

「你好，你有甚麼緊急情況？」話筒另一頭的女人問道。
「嗨，我現在跟一個小孩在一起，他說他爸爸死了。」
「好的，地址是？」

拐彎之後，我看見數輛閃著燈的車停泊在男孩的門前。

「看來已經有人報警了，抱歉浪費了你的時間。」
「不要緊。」女人說罷就掛線了。

我們走近男孩家的時候，他緊緊抓住我的手。

「孩子，不用擔心，一切都會好起來的。」

我們穿過那群醫護人員和正在詢問鄰居的警察，走近大門。

「你媽媽在裡面嗎？」我問。

He nodded again.

"Go inside and see her, I bet she's been wondering where you've been."

He disappeared inside the building.

"What's going on?" I asked a police officer as he approached me.
"Sir, this is a crime scene, you have to leave."
"Sorry, I'll get out of your way."

I stood on the pavement outside the front yard when a neighbour approached.

"It's so sad something like this can happen in this day and age," he said shaking his head mournfully.
"Heart attacks can strike at any moment; one minute you're here and the next you're gone," I replied trying to console him.
"It wasn't a heart attack. It appears their little boy just went crazy and stabbed his father to death. How do you wrap your head around that?"

My blood ran cold and my face drained of colour.

他又點點頭。

「進去找她吧，我想她應該也在找你吧。」

他走進建築物裡。

「發生甚麼事了？」一名警察走過來後我問他。
「先生，這是犯罪現場，你必須離開。」
「抱歉，我會離開的了。」

我站在前院外的行人道上，一個鄰居向我走過來。

「想不到這樣的悲劇竟然會在今天這個時代發生。」他搖搖頭，惋惜地說。
「心臟病隨時都可能發生，前一分鐘還好好的，下一分鐘就死掉了。」我試圖安慰他。
「不是心臟病發啊，好像是他們的小兒子突然發瘋了，把爸爸刺死了。咦，你怎麼抱著頭？」

頓時我體內的血液像凝結了般，臉色也慘白起來。

"Are you okay?" the man asked.
"Sir?"
"Uhh," was all I could muster.

It was then I heard the feminine screams from inside the house, and I knew what happened.

The boy reappeared at the threshold of the door, his t-shirt painted red, and said, "My mummy's dead."

「你還好吧？」男人問。
「先生？」
「呃⋯⋯」我只能吐出這樣的聲音。

然後我聽見了屋內傳出了女人的尖叫聲，我知道發生甚麼事了⋯⋯

男孩又出現在門檻前，上衣染紅了的他跟我說：「我媽媽死了。」

Beyond the Fence

I have lived here all my life and had no reason to leave. However my curiosity was piqued when I found the wooden fence behind a forest of trees. I couldn't tell Papa because he would send me to the basement. I instead asked my older sister.

"What's beyond the fence?"
She glared at me as she said, "Leave it alone. There's nothing past there."
"How would you know?" I asked.
Papa peeked in our room and said, "Quiet down...or else."

We knew the command and stayed quiet the rest of the night. As my older sister slept, I planned out my way to see beyond the fence. I could climb it at first and if that didn't work I could dig.

I had to be careful because if Papa knew what I was doing I might be in the basement where my other sisters were.

I waited until the sun rose before I slipped out of bed and went to the woods where I last saw the fence. I shimmied my way up and gritted my teeth as I felt splinters dig into my shin. I was up top and the only way down was to jump.

圍欄後面

我一出生就已經住在這裡，也沒有離開的理由。但當我發現森林後面有個木圍欄的時候，它完全激發了我的好奇心！可是我不可以告訴爸爸，因為他會把我關進地牢，於是我去問我的姐姐。

「圍欄後面有甚麼？」
她瞪著我說：「你別管，那裡甚麼都沒有。」
「你怎麼知道？」我問。
爸爸向我們的房間瞥了一眼說：「不要吵，不然……」

我們都清楚他的指令，所以剩下的時間都保持安靜。等到姐姐睡著了，我溜出去看看圍欄後面到底有甚麼。如果爬過去不行的話，那就挖地道吧。

我一定要非常小心，不然被爸爸發現的話，我就會跟其他姐姐一樣在地牢過活了。

我等到日出才溜下床，悄悄地走向森林，走到我上次看見圍欄的地方。有些碎屑掉進我屁股間，我打著哆嗦，咬緊牙關一直向前走。走到了一個位置，那裡很高，要前進我只好跳下去。

I jumped and looked around. So many colors! The grass was softer and the air was more fresh. I looked at the fence and smiled. I was beyond the fence.

My smiled vanished when I saw that the fence held posters with my face on them with the title in bold reading 'missing child'.

我跳了下去，然後到處張望。是個色彩繽紛的地方！這裡的草更軟，空氣更清新。我帶笑回望著圍欄。我在圍欄後面了！

但我的笑容很快消失了。我看到圍欄上貼著一張海報，上面有我的樣子，大大的標題寫著「失蹤小孩」。

Hog Body

I love school and I'm told that that is a bad thing. I say told but they are not the type of kids that use words, but fists and spit and wedgies.

They call me Hog Body because I am fat and that too is a bad thing. They are bigger than me, but not fat. They're bigger as in older, they're in seventh grade and they tower over me like elephants. I am just a third-grader and they make me cry and bleed and they broke my nose one time.

When I'm alone in my room, reading, and fantasizing about standing up to them I call them the Elephants and I, Hog Body, win the battle with the things I've learned in school. I love history the most. Hannibal used elephants in war, I learned that in history class. But Hannibal's enemies had pigs, and they learned that if you covered a pig in fat and set them on fire they made the elephants freak out and then the elephants got set on fire too and they died.

Mommy's drunk and daddy's gone and I have matches and I cook for mommy when she's drunk sometimes so I have oil from the kitchen and I'm at school now. Ms. Adams asks why I'm in their classroom and then she screams.

I smell like bacon as I run towards the Elephants.

Author: Tanja Simone

肥豬

我很愛學校，但常常有人告訴我學校是不好的東西。雖然説是「告訴」我，但他們不是那種用言語來教導人的孩子，他們用的是拳頭、口水和鞋跟。

他們叫我做「肥豬」，因為我很胖，胖也是不好的東西。他們都比我高大，但不胖。因為他們年紀都比我大，所以比我高。他們是七年級生，所以像大象群般，比我高很多。我只是個三年級生，他們把我弄哭、弄得我流血，有一次還弄斷了我的鼻子。

我獨自在房間的時候，會邊看書邊幻想在他們面前站起來，我叫他們做「象群」，而我「肥豬」就憑在學校習得的知識戰勝了象群。我最愛歷史科了。我在歷史課學會了著名軍事家漢尼拔就是用大象來打仗。但漢尼拔的敵人用豬來反擊，他們學懂把脂肪塗在豬身上然後燃起來，就可以嚇壞那些大象，然後那些大象都會燒著然後死掉。

媽媽喝醉了，爸爸不在家，我也準備好火柴。有時媽媽喝醉了我要幫忙煮飯，所以我在廚房拿了點油。我現在在學校，Adams 老師問我為甚麼在他們的課室出現之後就失聲尖叫。

然後我散發著煙肉的香氣衝向象群。

Imagination Land

I've been able to read minds since I was a child. It's not really like how you see in the movies, though. It's not like listening to the radio. It's much more immersive. I experience everything as if I'm really there. It's a thrilling experience when you read the right minds. The trouble is really with finding minds worth reading.

Frankly, reading adults is as fun as doing taxes. Kids' minds, on the other hand, are amazing. They're not bogged down with work and stress and dissatisfaction. The mind of a child is filled with imagination and adventure. That's why I became a kindergarten teacher.

I sit at my desk and watch as my class colors. I smile as they doodle away with their crayons. I reach out and peek into their minds. In an instant, I take off with Carlos in a rocket ship, hurtling past swirling galaxies. I visit far-off planets full of blob-like aliens and two-headed martians. I smile and move on to Marcy. I can smell the candy canes and jelly beans as I'm pulled into a veritable candyland, complete with gumdrop castles and caramel waterfalls. She plays hopscotch with gingerbread men, giggling her musical little laugh.

I'm about to move on to Thomas when I feel a tug at my dress. I look down to see Sarah. She's one of the most adorable little girls I've ever seen. Beautiful brown curls, big

想像樂園

我小時候就有讀心的能力了，但跟你在電影裡看到的不同。那不像是聽收音機般，而是更加擬真的感覺，就像我真的親臨其境一樣。當你讀心讀得對的時候，就會是一個令人興奮的體驗。但要找到一個值得讀的心才是難事。

坦白說，讀大人的思緒就像和做稅一樣有趣。另一方面，孩子的思緒也是很有趣的，他們不會因工作壓力和不滿而陷入困境。孩子的思緒充滿了想像和冒險。這就是我成為幼稚園老師的原因。

我坐在教師桌上，看著我的學生在填顏色。看著他們用蠟筆塗鴉時，我都會會心微笑。我走進了他們的思緒去看個究竟。在一瞬間，我坐在 Carlos 的火箭上一同起飛，衝破了一個又一個星空漩渦，之後到訪了遙遠的星球，那裡有很多水滴型外星人和雙頭火星人。我微笑著走到 Marcy 的思緒，我被拉進一個名副其實的糖果天地，我聞到拐杖糖和豆豆糖的香味，還看到橡皮糖城堡和焦糖瀑布。她跟薑餅人一起玩跳飛機，她咯咯的笑聲像音樂般動聽。

我打算走到 Thomas 那邊時，感覺到有人在扯我的裙子。我低下頭，看到了 Sarah。她是我見過的最可愛的小女孩之一，她有著美麗的棕色捲髮、像小狗般惹人憐愛的眼睛和閃閃發光的笑容。

puppy dog eyes, and a gleaming smile.

"Miss Dupree, I made this for you!" she exclaims, handing me a paper. I take it from her and see myself in stick figure form. "I Luv Ms. Dooprv" is scrawled across the top in multiple colors.

"I love it!" I exclaim and give her a great big hug.

Sarah's only been with the class for a couple days and I have yet to have a peek at her hopes and dreams. I reach out and touch her mind. And I nearly vomit.

I choke as I'm hit with wave after wave of the hot, fetid stench of death. My mind's eye is blinded by a darkness which seems almost alive, spilling into my brain, seeking to blot out everything it touches. In the void, I feel slimy coils roiling around me, wrapping around my legs, pressing against my face, a gigantic beast hungrily probing the darkness in search for food. And then a keening wail rises up, nearly bursting my eardrums. The screams of thousands of souls, crying out in sorrow. Crying out for death.

And then I'm back in the classroom. I let go of Sarah and compose myself, hoping she can't see me shaking.

「Dupree 老師，我畫了這個給你！」她高聲說，把一張紙遞給我。我接過來，看見自己變成了火柴人的模樣，她用不同的顏色筆在畫紙頂部寫著潦草的「我艾 Doopry 老師」。

「我很喜歡！」我大叫著，然後給她一個大大的擁抱。

因為 Sarah 只上了幾天的課，我還沒有窺探她的希望和夢想。於是我走進了她的思緒，但那幾乎讓我吐了出來。

一波又一波熾熱、散發著惡臭的死亡氣息衝擊著我，使我感到窒息。我的思緒好像被有生命的黑暗蒙蔽著，一直蔓延至我的腦袋，想要佔據它能觸及的一切。在空虛中，我感覺有些黏滑的線圈在我身邊流竄著，它們更繞著我的雙腿、壓在我的臉上。還有一隻在黑暗中尋找食物的巨型野獸。然後一陣哭喪聲響起，尖得幾乎弄穿我的耳膜。數以千計的靈魂在悲傷中、死亡中哭喊著。

然後我回到了教室。我放開了 Sarah，使自己冷靜下來，希望她沒有看見我在發抖。

"That's a lovely picture, Sarah," I say, nearly whispering. "Now go along and get ready for snack time, alright?"

She nods happily and skips off. I watch her as she goes. The minds of children are the most wonderful thing in the universe.

But whatever that thing in the blue dress is, it is no child.

「Sarah，你畫得很好呢，」我以悄悄話的聲浪說著：「現在過去等待點心時間吧，好嗎？」

她愉快地點頭，然後跑跳著走了。我看著她的背影，想著孩子的思緒是宇宙中最美妙的事物。

但是無論那個穿著藍色裙子的是甚麼鬼東西也好，都不是個孩子。

Fourteen isn't All it's Cracked Up to Be

Today was almost exactly the same as yesterday. Supposedly though, today was "special," since Alice was turning fourteen. Alice didn't feel any different, yet she was sure she would be met with new responsibilities, new duties, new ways to describe "boring". The birthday girl in question, was sitting alone at a table at the edge of her lawn, contemplating why her birthday wasn't happy. Why she wasn't happy. The main reason, or reasons, were running around, screeching and laughing, all over the tackily decorated lawn: the brats. All of her friends were on one vacation or another, while she was stuck at home; it was just her luck that her birthday fell on Spring Break this year. The only girl even remotely around her age was twelve, and she was making sure her three pesky younger brothers didn't kill the other guests. Alice sighed. She didn't even ask for this party.

Indeed, Alice was mulling this over at her worst party ever, when to her surprise, a fat rabbit ran up to her.

"Why so glum, huh? It's your birthday, after all."
Alice looked up to see if she had heard correctly. "Did you just speak?"
"Of course I did. All rabbits can speak, y'know."
"Can they? I'm fourteen now; I'm supposed to stop believing in fairy tales and magic and start being a grown-up."
The rabbit shook his head, tsking. "Fourteen sounds like it's

Alice 的生日會

今天與昨天幾乎完全沒有不同，不過，今天是個「特別日子」，因為是 Alice 的十四歲生日。Alice 也不覺得自己有甚麼不同，但她確信自己將會有新的責任、新的職責和用來形容「無聊」的新方式。壽星女坐在草坪邊的一張桌子上，沉思著為甚麼她的生日不快樂，為甚麼自己不快樂。那些小伙子在殘破不堪的裝飾草坪上到處跑著、尖叫著和笑著，他們就是那些導致 Alice 不快樂的主要原因了。她的所有朋友都在放假，而她就只困在家裡；或只是她不幸，今年她的生日剛好是春假。那些小伙子裡面只有一個跟 Alice 年紀相若的女孩，十二歲的她正在確保她那三個討厭的弟弟沒有殺死其他客人。Alice 嘆了口氣，她根本不想要這個生日會。

Alice 在她最糟糕的生日會反覆想著這個念頭，突然一隻胖兔子跑到她身邊，讓她吃了一驚。

「喂喂，為何苦著臉呢？畢竟是你的生日啊。」
Alice 抬起頭，以為自己聽錯：「你剛才說話嗎？」
「當然是啦，所有兔子都會說話啊。」
「真的嗎？但我現在十四歲了，我不應該再相信甚麼童話和魔法之類的了，我要做大人了。」
兔子搖搖頭：「十四歲聽起來好像沒甚麼好玩的。」
「嗯……」Alice 嘆了口氣。
兔子想到了甚麼，耳朵豎了起來：「呃，不如我帶你到我家，

no fun at all."
"It's not," Alice sighed.
The rabbit's ears perked up as he thought of something. "Say, why don't I take you back to my home? There's lots of fun to be had there!" Alice glanced back at the unruly crowd of children her parents had invited over against her wishes. Then, she turned back towards the rabbit, her decision made.
"Sure, why not?"
"Follow me," he said, and took off into the underbrush.

Alice struggled to chase after the creature, with it's speed and size allowing to traverse the dense environment easily. Alice didn't even look behind her as the sounds of the party got further and further away. Then, the pair stopped in a clearing in front of a deep, foreboding hole.

"What are you waiting for? Jump in."
"Are you sure this is okay? I won't get hurt or anything?"
"When you jump in, you'll float down, like magic. Promise."
"Okay..." And jump Alice did.

The red and blue police lights illuminated the front lawn of Alice's residence as her parents stood worriedly in its front entrance, conversing with the officer man.

那裡有很多好玩的東西！」

Alice 回頭看了一下那群不守規矩的小孩，是她父母請來的，但 Alice 並不喜歡他們。然後，她轉身向著兔子，下了決定：
「嗯！好啊！」
「跟著我。」牠説罷就向灌木叢跑走了。

Alice 吃力地追著牠，始終兔子的速度和大小讓牠可以輕鬆地穿過密集的叢林。雖然從生日會那邊發出的聲音愈來愈遠，但 Alice 也沒有回頭看。然後，Alice 和兔子在一個有著不祥預感的深洞前面停了下來。

「你還等甚麼？跳進去吧。」
「你確定這樣沒問題嗎？我不會受傷或是怎樣嗎？」
「當你跳進去的時候，你會像有魔法一樣浮起來，我保證。」
「好吧……」然後 Alice 就跳了進去。

紅藍交替的警燈照亮了 Alice 家前面的草坪，她的父母一臉擔憂地站在前門，與警員交談著。

"We'll try our hardest to find your daughter," he assured them. "Now, was she doing anything that seemed out of the ordinary before she ran off?"
The mother replied with a unsure tone about her voice. "Um, I'm not certain- I only saw it for a moment- but I think Alice was sitting at the edge of the lawn, all alone, even though it was her party."
"Anything else, ma'am?"
"Yes- I think she was talking to herself."

「我們會竭盡所能把你的女兒找回來，」警員向他們保證：「那麼，她在逃跑之前有沒有發生甚麼不尋常的事？」

她母親猶豫地回答：「呃，我不太確定……我只看到一陣子……雖然這是她的生日會……但我想那時 Alice 自己一個人坐了在草坪邊。」

「還有其他嗎？」

「有的……我想她是在跟自己講話。」

There's a Monster Under My Bed

I can hear it every night. I told mom and dad too, but they don't believe me. They went in my room, daddy went under the bed and even acted like someone grabbed his feet for a moment, and then laughed it off. They told me there's no monsters in real life, and if there were, they would be friendly monsters like in that movie Monsters Inc. But I kept insisting and they got mad. I heard them talking about me outside our apartment, saying they shouldn't come when I cry about monsters, saying that I'll never learn if they do. So I didn't call them that night, 'cause I knew they wouldn't come. But the noise did. It always did.

I was almost asleep, very late in the night. It was right under my bed. First a very small crying noise. If the floor was thicker I wouldn't even hear it. Then the steps, loud and uneven, stumbling, probably right outside the room. Then a terrifying squeak, a door being pushed. And a crying voice, a child's voice, would say "No daddy, please not today".

And then the monster spoke, and it was the only thing he would ever say:
"Shut up".

Author: Gabriel Oro

我床底下有怪物

我每晚都聽見它講話。我跟爸爸媽媽說過，但他們不相信我。他們來過我的房間，爸爸鑽到床下，一會兒還裝作有人抓住他的腳，然後又一笑置之。他們告訴我現實生活中沒有怪獸，如果真的有怪獸，也會像電影《怪獸公司》裡的怪獸般友善。但我一直堅持真的有怪獸，他們就生氣了。我聽到他們在公寓外面討論我的事，說他們不應該在我哭鬧說有怪獸時過來安慰我，因為這樣會使我永遠學不乖。所以那晚我沒有叫爸爸媽媽過來，因為我知道他們也不會過來。但那些聲音會來，就像平時一樣。

當時已經很晚了，我快睡著了。它就在我床底下出現。首先傳來一陣非常微弱的哭泣聲，微弱得如果地板再厚一點我就不會聽見了。接著是一陣蹣跚、響亮、沒有規律的腳步聲，可能正正在房間外面。然後是駭人的「吱」一聲，門被推開了。接著一把哭聲，一把屬於小孩的聲音，就會說：「爸爸不要……今天不要好嗎……」。

然後那怪獸開口說話了，也是他唯一會說的：
「閉嘴。」

I Caught My Daughter Drowning the Cat Today

When I arrived home, I put my shopping on the counter and peered out the window to see my daughter Kerry wrestling with the cat.

I opened the back door and heard her shout, "Shut up Mr. Kitty, why won't you just shut up."

I ran down the garden path and saw the poor animal squirm, thrashing against my daughter's grip; his razor sharp claws leaving behind fine red marks on her wrists and arms that oozed blood.

By the time I arrived she had let go of the family pet, which floated lifeless in the bucket of water. She breathed heavily and glared at the animal, satisfied it had now shut up.

She turned and looked up at me, "My arms hurt, mummy."

Somewhat numb, I ignored her and picked up the body and walked back to the house.

"Mummy?" my daughter asked inquisitively.

She is sitting at the kitchen table now. She winces as I dab the iodine soaked cotton wool to her wounds. She doesn't speak. She appears unfazed by what she's done. I am careful not to

我發現女兒把家貓淹死了

當我回到家時，我將買回來的東西放在吧檯上，望出窗外，看到女兒 Kerry 在跟貓咪打架。

我打開後門，聽見她大叫著：「閉嘴，貓貓先生，你為甚麼不閉嘴？」

我沿著花園的路跑過去，只見那可憐的貓咪扭動著身體，用力地從女兒的緊握中掙脫。牠鋒利如剃刀的爪子在她的手腕和手臂上留下了細微的紅色痕跡，滲出了血液。

當我到達時，她沒有再緊握著貓咪，因為牠已在水桶裡浮了起來。她喘著氣，瞪著那隻動物，對於牠現在已經閉嘴了覺得很滿意。

她轉過頭看著我：「媽媽，我的手受傷了。」

我有點驚呆了，無視了她，拾起了那屍體，然後向屋子走去。

「媽媽？」我女兒一臉好奇地問。

她現在坐在廚房的桌子上。我把泡了碘的藥棉輕拍著她的傷口，痛得她齜牙咧嘴。她沒有說話，但她似乎對自己剛剛做

be too hard on her.

"Honey, do you know why you did what you did?" I ask.

She shakes her head gently, as if she didn't understand herself.

"Mr. Kitty wouldn't shut up," she complains, looking at the cat that lays lifeless in its bed.

I rub her arms before asking again. She absentmindedly stares at the far wall, at the paintings that adorn it.

"Why did you think that was okay?"
"Daddy does it that way."
"What do you mean?"
"I saw him telling Jason to shut up, before he took him out for ice cream."

I drop the cotton wool and kneel down in front of her.

"Sweetie, when was this? It's important," I ask, my anxiety turning to panic.

"This afternoon, in the bathroom. Jason was very quiet after that, I think he fell asleep. Then he took him out for ice

的事毫不畏懼。我很謹慎，不想對她太嚴厲。

「親愛的，你為甚麼做了那樣的事呢？」我問。

她輕輕地搖了搖頭，好像不明白自己在想甚麼。

「貓貓先生不閉嘴。」她看著躺在貓床上毫無生氣的貓咪抱怨著。

再問她之前，我揉揉她的手臂。她漫不經心地盯著釘在遠處牆上的裝飾畫。

「你為甚麼覺得那樣是對的事呢？」
「爸爸也這樣做。」
「這是甚麼意思？」
「我看見他帶 Jason 出去吃冰淇淋之前叫他閉嘴。」

我放下藥棉，跪在她前面。

「親愛的，那是甚麼時候？這很重要的。」我邊問邊感到原本的焦慮開始變成恐慌。

「今天下午，在浴室裡。在那之後 Jason 很安靜，我想他應

cream and I cried because he wouldn't take me. That's when Mr. Kitty started whining. That made me angry and I wanted him to shut up, just like Daddy does."

She sighs with her shoulders.

"Daddy says you should run yourself a bath. He's got something very special planned for us this evening."

該是睡著了。然後爸爸就帶 Jason 出去吃冰淇淋了，我哭了，因為他不帶我去。就是那個時候貓貓先生開始哀鳴著，這讓我生氣了，所以我想讓他閉嘴，就像爸爸對 Jason 一樣。」

她聳聳肩，嘆了口氣。

「爸爸說你應該好好泡個澡，他說他今晚準備了一些很特別的東西給我們。」

Vexed Confession
惱 人 自 白

And I Was Childfree No More

Maternal instinct – how I once loathed the concept.

If the impetus to pop out babies was in every woman's wiring, then I must have been a different model entirely. I'd always thought that my best friend, Sarah, felt likewise – until she went and got herself knocked up. She promised me that things would still be the same after the baby came, but I knew it was a lie. That screaming, crying infant was going to ruin everything. I was so certain that my own, fabled maternal instinct would never arrive.

But then Sarah had her baby.

Seeing Jacob in the hospital for the first time, I knew at once that I had been wrong. It seems, motherhood actually was for me. Suddenly, I could feel that primal surge of love and desire that parents carried on about in movies. Those gem blue eyes, that rich brown hair; he would be perfect. From that moment on, I knew that if I ever wanted to have a child, I would need to make Jacob a part of my family. I was going to be a mother, no matter what.

Over the years, I kept a close watch over Jacob. Sarah leaned on me heavily for help with raising him, and I complied all too willingly. My uterus ached every time I saw the boy. There Sarah would be, absentmindedly parenting him, so

我不再沒兒沒女

母性本能——我曾經很厭惡這個概念。

如果生兒育女是每個女人的必備設定，那麼我一定是完全不同的構造。我一直認為我最好的朋友 Sarah 也是這樣想的，直到她的肚子被搞大了。她答應我，就算寶寶出生之後，甚麼都不會變，但是我知道那是個謊言，那個尖聲哭泣的嬰兒將會破壞一切。我確信，傳說中的母性本能永遠不會降臨在我身上。

直到 Sarah 的寶寶出生了。

第一次在醫院看到 Jacob 的時候，我就知道我一直都錯了。原來母性一直都在。突然間，我感覺到那些父母看電影時會出現的愛和慾望，那些本能如浪潮般湧現。那雙寶石般的藍色眼睛、亮麗的棉色頭髮，他會是個完美人選。從那刻開始，我知道如果我想要一個孩子，就要視 Jacob 為我家的一分子。我無論如何也會成為一位母親。

這些年來，我都密切地關注著 Jacob。撫養 Jacob 的日子裡，Sarah 很依賴我，我也很樂意幫忙。每次看到這個男孩，我的子宮都會隱隱作痛。因為 Sarah 總是心不在焉的養育他，完全不知道上天給了她一份多珍貴的禮物。我總是忍著不說出口，但是還是極度渴望她會徹底消失。只有這樣我才

completely unaware of the gift she had been given. I always bit my tongue, but longed desperately to get her out of the way, once and for all. Only then could I finally be a mother.

My wish eventually came true when Jacob was sixteen; Sarah was killed after a nasty fall down the stairs. It was such an unusual way for her to die and yet, no one was suspicious.

Custody was a foregone conclusion. Jacob's father was long out of the picture, and I had served as Jacob's godmother since he was born. The judge quickly appointed me his legal guardian. In a few days, Jacob is going to come and live with me. After all this waiting, I'll soon have my dream – I'm finally going to experience motherhood. It's a bit late in life to undertake, but so many mid–30s women start now. Fate will, at long last, bring me my child.

Jacob is going to make a great father for them.

能成為一位母親。

當 Jacob 十六歲時，我的美夢終於成真了，因為 Sarah 失足跌下樓梯死了。雖然她的死法很奇怪，但沒有人懷疑過。

我早已料到 Jacob 的撫養權會判給誰。Jacob 的父親一早已不知所終，而自從他出生以來，我就一直擔任教母的角色。所以法官很快就委任我為 Jacob 的法定監護人。幾天之後，Jacob 就要和我一起生活。等了那麼久，我終於可以實現我的夢想——終於可以體驗當母親的感覺了！雖然可能有點遲，但現在也有很多女人三十多歲才開始當母親。命運最終也會為我帶來孩子。

Jacob 將會是個好爸爸。

OCD

I have obsessive–compulsive disorder. I'm not a germaphobe or a checker, I just really hate odd numbers. It's hard to explain, I just don't feel right and I have to rectify it. I see one shoe on the floor, I have to find the other before the anxiety becomes unbearable. I buy food in pairs. I have two cars, even though I only use one.

I was so delighted when my kids were born and I had twins, identical ones at that. They were the light of my life, and for the longest time I got my OCD under control. It's amazing how the love of someone you created can change the way you think about things. How silly I was to think something as arbitrary as odd numbers could rule my life. Thank God for the miracle of life.

When my daughter Sally became sick with Pneumonia, it sent me into depression. I watched as my sweet little child withered away. I sat on the chair next to her bed when the nurse came along and pulled the sheet over her face.

Looking at the linen pulled taught over my daughter's face, my leg started jittering. A cold sweat gathered on my brow.

I hate odd numbers.

What do I do with the other one.

Author: Edwin Crowe

強迫症

我是個強迫症患者。我不是潔癖，也不是要不斷重複檢查的那種患者，我只是極度討厭單數。我很難解釋，總之一看到單數就會渾身不對勁，一定要把它矯正好才行。例如我看到地上只有一隻鞋子，我一定要把另一隻都找出來我才能放鬆。所以我買食物會成雙成對地買，車子也是，雖然我只駕一台，但也買了兩台。

當我的孩子出生時我超開心的！因為她們是雙胞胎，還是同卵雙生的那種！她們就像是我生命中的明燈，也使我長期以來的強迫症得到控制。我親自創造的小寶貝竟然改變了自己過往對事物的看法，真的很奇妙！我還以為單數這種蠢事會控制我的人生，我真是太傻了。感謝上帝為我帶來奇蹟。

但當我的女兒 Sally 感染了肺炎後，也使我患上了抑鬱症。我眼巴巴的看著我那甜美的小寶貝消失了。我坐在她床邊的椅子上，看著護士進來把白布蓋過她的臉。

麻布下隱約透露著 Sally 的面容，我的雙腿不禁抖動起來。一抹冷汗集結在我的眉心。

我討厭單數。

落單了的那個我該怎樣處置她……

The Story Ends with a Double Murder

"Once upon a time, there lived a beggar with a nail embedded in his foot. He had a small puppy who went everywhere with him. The two of them were very happy together, but the nail was hurting the beggar a lot. One day, he went to the doctor to remove it, but to their astonishment, the nail had grown in size!"

"The doctor told the beggar that removing the nail now would be extremely painful, so the beggar left it in. The only problem was that the nail began to cause him more pain when he walked, and he would bleed often. To deal with this, the beggar had set his puppy down instead of carrying it, and had to watch as his poor puppy injured its feet on the rough concrete."

"In a month's time, after the first consultation, the nail grew so large, it pierced into his ankles. The poor beggar was in so much pain that he couldn't walk, only shuffle, and the doctor told him that it was too late for him to remove it. The puppy's feet were also scratched and bleeding, and it was difficult for it to walk. The beggar now had to carry it, and its weight caused him even more pain."

I paused in my story, listening carefully. In the other room, I could hear my husband snoring loudly. I sighed in relief.

雙重謀殺的結局

「很久很久以前，有一個腳上刺著釘子的乞丐，他有一隻跟著他到處走的小狗。他們很開心的走在一起，但釘子害得乞丐很痛，於是有一天，他去了看醫生，打算把釘子拔掉。但令人驚訝的是，釘子竟然增長了！」

「醫生告訴乞丐，現在去除釘子會非常非常痛苦，所以乞丐就由它留在腳上，沒有拔掉。但這樣有個問題，釘子會讓他走路時更痛苦，而且也會經常流血。為了解決這個問題，乞丐得把小狗放下，不再抱著牠，不得不看著可憐的小狗走在粗糙的混凝土上，弄傷了腳。」

「離第一次會診之後一個月，釘子變成大得刺進了乞丐的腳踝。可憐的他受了很大的痛苦，不能走路，只能拖著腿走。醫生告訴他，現在想除掉釘子已經太遲了。小狗的腳也被刮傷和流血，走路很困難。乞丐現在要抱著他，而牠的重量使他更加痛苦。」

我暫停了故事，細心地聆聽著。在另一個房間裡，傳出了丈夫大大的鼻鼾聲，我鬆了口氣。

"Why doesn't he just pull out the nail from the start, mommy?" asked my son curiously, his innocent wide eyes looking up at me. "And why does he carry his dog even though it hurts him?"

I smiled at him, choking back tears, as he hugged my arms. My bruises were well hidden underneath my long sleeves, and I could just manage to resist whimpering. "I don't know, sweetheart. Now go to sleep."

「媽媽，那為甚麼他不一早把釘子拔掉呢？」兒子好奇地問，用他天真無邪的眼睛望著我：「小狗弄痛了他，乞丐為甚麼還抱著牠呢？」

他抱著我的手臂，我微笑，強忍著眼淚。衣服的長袖子完美地掩蓋著我的瘀傷，我只能按捺著，不讓自己哭出來：「我不知道呢親愛的，現在去睡覺吧。」

Bird Bath

I was never too much of a handful as a child. Or at least I like to think I wasn't. I didn't do too much outside of playing with my dollhouse or looking for bugs in the backyard. I remember we had a stone birdbath that was just always there, even from before we moved there.

Often, I'd take a bug, like an ant, or a rolly polly, and drop it into the middle of the bath and just watch. Sometimes they would spin helplessly in the center before they drowned, but other times they would struggle just right and manage to swim their way to the edge.

I always had a small admiration for the insects that were smart enough to do that. Not that it made me merciful. Because I would always gently blow right back into the water and watched them finish drowning. I didn't have a reason for it. I think that's what scares me the most right now.

Because right now my arms are getting tired. And no matter how many times I reach the shores edge, something keeps pushing me back to the center of the lake…

Author: Atlani Godina

鳥澡盆

我小時候不算是個讓人頭痛的小孩，或者説我比較偏好覺得自己不是。我不常走到外面玩娃娃屋，也很少到後園找蟲子。我記得當時後園有一個石製、供鳥兒戲水的澡盆，它在我們搬過來之前已經存在了。

我不時會抓隻蟲子，像是螞蟻或是牛屎蟲，把牠們丟到澡盆中間，然後望著牠們。有時候牠們會無助地在中央旋轉，然後溺死，但其他時候牠們會努力掙扎，向澡盆邊緣游過去。

我一直很佩服這些昆蟲那麼聰明，但這並沒有使我變得仁慈。我每次都會向牠們輕輕地吹氣，令牠們回到水裡，然後望著牠們慢慢溺死。我這樣做並沒有特別的原因，我認為這是最令我驚訝的事情。我想這也是現在最令我恐慌的事。

因為現在我手臂開始累了，無論我努力游向岸邊多少次也好，總有些東西把我推回湖的中央⋯⋯

Click 'Yes' to Send

My fingers are moving at lightspeed — scrolling, selecting, clicking, over and over. So many names to go over. It makes me wish that people could quit dying so often. It doesn't help that until my shift is over, I'm basically lording over five whole regions — albeit small regions, but lots of people die every day. I can't afford to be late for the start of my shift, or things begin piling up. So I appear at computer 52807 every evening at eight, local Death time.

I pause for a second to scratch at my neck – damn these uncomfortable company uniforms – and my hand flies back to my mouse. **"Which Afterlife Program will you send —— to?"** I click an option, and **"Are you sure?"** Yup. **"Click 'Yes' to send,"** Yadda, yadda, yadda. The clicking never ceases in this room, and the headphones I'm required to wear do nothing to muffle the noise. Indeed, the same old, same old, until—

Beep

I've got a call.

A man's voice screeches into my headphones. "I–I was told I could talk to a professional!?"
"Yes that's me. Is there anything you'd like to do to improve your pre–selected Afterlife Program?" I recite automatically.

按「確認」以發送

我用手指飛快地在滾動、選擇、點擊，重複又重複。好多名字要仔細檢查呢……這讓我不想那麼多人死去，直到我的值班時間結束前我也是這樣想的。基本上我在管轄五個完整地區，儘管那些都是小地區，但是每天也有很多人死去。我不能遲到，否則就會有很多東西開始堆積起來。所以我每天晚上都會在「死亡時區」的八時登入 52807 號電腦。

我暫停了一下，抓抓脖子，該死的公司制服讓我很不舒服，然後又將手放回到滑鼠上。「**你要將……送到哪個來生計劃？**」我點擊一個選項，「**你確定嗎？**」是的。「**點擊『確認』以發送。**」諸如此類的。這個房間永遠都充斥著點擊的聲音，而公司要我戴著的耳機也不能消除噪音。還是老樣子，還是老樣子，直到……

嗶

有電話打來。

一把男人的聲音颼入我的耳機：「有人跟我說這裡可以和專業人士交談，對吧？」
「是的，那就是我。您需要改善已預選的來生計劃嗎？」我倒背如流。

"Yes! Pl–Please! I don't wanna go to Hell!"

"But Mr. Harlem Walker sir," I reply. "Your records show that you've murdered and raped approximately thirty–seven girls. The Heaven Program is unavailable to you."

"Wh–What about purgatory?"

"The Purgatory Program is only available to subjects with Earthly attachments, and you have none."

"Please! There has to be something! Anything! What about reincarnation?"

"Completely out of the question," I say with a smirk. My eyes flick to a pop–up notification. "It seems you're in luck, sir. A position has just opened up."

"A position? Where?"

"We here at Afterlife Placement Co. have an international medical wing where souls like you can be reattached to a physical organ donor. The best part is," I cheerfully say, "Once an organ is donated, it grows back, so you can keep donating and donating. Participation for fifty years results on your name being placed on the Redemption Program wait–list! So, will you fill up that spot, Mr. Harlem Walker?"

"Will it hurt?" I don't even bother sugarcoating it.

"It sure will," I chirp, my voice cheerier than ever.

"I–I don't want to then! Please! Anything but that!" Filthy coward, I think, but keep it to myself.

"Anything?"

"ANYTHING!"

「是的！拜、拜託！我不想去地獄！」

「Harlem Walker 先生，但是，」我回答。「記錄顯示您已經強姦及殺害了大約三十七個女孩。天堂計劃是不適用的。」

「那、那煉獄呢？」

「煉獄計劃只適用於有『塵世』附件的對象，但先生您沒有。」

「拜託！一定還有其他計劃的！對吧！那輪迴呢？」

「絕對不可能，」我假笑地說著。我眼睛瞥去了一個彈出通知視窗：「先生，您走運了，剛剛有個位置開放了。」

「有個位置？哪裡？」

「我們來生安置公司有一個國際醫療分支，像你這樣的靈魂可以重新連接到另一個器官捐贈者身上，而最棒的部分是，」我高興地說：「捐贈了器官之後，它會重新長出來，所以你可以繼續捐贈再捐贈，參加五十年的話，您的名字就可以列入救贖計劃的等待名單！所以 Harlem Walker 先生，你要參加來填補那個空缺嗎？」

「會痛嗎？」

我甚至不打算婉轉地說：「肯定會的。」我興奮地尖聲說。

「那、那我不想要了！拜託！除此之外甚麼都好！」

污穢的懦夫，我心裡想著，但沒有說出口。

「甚麼都好？」

「甚、麼、都、好！」

"Well sir, it seems that Hell just so happens to fit under 'anything but that!' "

The pop–up appears. **"Which Afterlife Program will you send Harlem Thomas Walker to?"** I click on **'Hell.'** **"Send Harlem Thomas Walker to Hell Program?"** I click **'Yes.'**

"WHAT THE HELL IS THAT!? OH GOD!!!!! HELP, SOMEONE!!! HEL–"

The **"Call has ended"** notification appears on my screen. "Idiot," I mutter. "There are other people waiting in line, you selfish bastard." I resume my selecting and clicking, focusing on the sea of names and faces. I check the time. Five minutes 'til four AM.

Thank god.

「好吧先生，似乎地獄就是『除此之外甚麼都好！』的選擇了。」

彈出窗口出現了：「**你要將** Harlem Thomas Walker **送到哪裡？**」我點擊「**地獄**」。「**發送** Harlem Thomas Walker **到地獄計劃？**」我點擊「**確認**」。

「這是甚麼鬼啊！啊，上帝啊！！！幫幫忙，有人嗎？？幫——」

「**通話已結束**」通知出現在我的屏幕上。「傻子，」我喃喃自語：「還有其他人在排隊等候呢，你這個自私的混蛋。」

我繼續選擇和點擊，專注在這片充滿名字和面孔的海洋。我看看時間，還有五分鐘才到凌晨四點鐘。

謝天謝地。

Forty–Eight is Waiting

My parents are perfectionists. For as long as I can remember they've both been obsessed with having everything just right. They're not shy about it either. They'll tell you right away when you're doing something less than perfect. They expect nothing less.

That's why I exist.

You see, my mother's job and educational background have provided her with the tools and knowledge to make sure that any child she has is absolutely perfect. She's had to do some of her own research, of course, but our basement laboratory makes that more attainable than for most.

There have been many failed attempts at perfection. My mother has never hidden that from me. I mean, it's right there in my name: Forty–Seven. The forty–seventh attempt at perfection. The "mes" before me each had a flaw, be it physical, emotional, mental, or behavioral. Sometimes they went for years without revealing them. Sometimes it was apparent from the beginning. But in every case, they had to be redone.

My mother isn't a monster, though. Each child is recycled, their parts (at least the ones without defect) reused so that the child may live on in some small way.

四十八正在等待

我的父母是完美主義者。我印象中他們倆都很執重於一切事物都要剛好，但當你做事做得不完美時，他們不會覺得不好意思，他們會馬上告訴你，因為他們不接受任何差池。

這就是我存在的原因。

你知道吧，我母親的工作和教育背景為她提供了工具和知識，以確保她所有的孩子是絕對完美的。當然，她需要自己做一些研究，但是我們地下室的實驗室有充足的設備，能幫她完成實驗。

為了追求完美，出現過很多的失敗品，但我的母親從來不會對我隱瞞。我是說，我的名字已經很明顯了，我叫「四十七」。第四十七次追求完美的實驗品。在我之前的都是有缺陷的，包括肉體上、情感上、精神上及行為上的缺陷。有時這些缺陷很多年也沒有顯露出來，有時一開始就已經顯而易見。但在每一種情況下，都必須要重做。

但我媽媽不是怪物，她會回收每個孩子，重新使用他們的部分（至少是那些沒有缺陷的部分），使那個孩子能以這樣一個小小的方式繼續活著。

Myself, I was "born" at age eight, created from the remnants of Forty–Six, who talked back and threw a tantrum at the mall. Forty–Six was created from Forty–Five, who developed a stutter. It goes all the way back like that. All the way to One, who was stillborn at twenty–eight weeks.

You might think it strange that my parents would tell me all of this, but I think it's generous. If I know where my predecessors have failed, I can be watchful of those same flaws in myself. I've made it almost to adulthood through my vigilance.

There's something that worries me, however. Lately I've been getting migraines. They start out with an aura of color, shifting through my vision and blinding me, and they follow with incapacitating pain. The first one happened at school, and I had to beg the nurse not to send me home sick. The second one happened at a sleepover party, and I spent the night hiding under the blankets.

I can't hide it forever, though. One day soon my parents will find out. On that day, Forty–Eight will be waiting.

而我「出生」時已經八歲，由四十六的殘餘物合併而成，他是個會頂嘴的人，更曾在商場發脾氣。而四十六就是由四十五造成，因為四十五有口吃。如此類推，一直去到那個在二十八周時就胎死腹中的一。

你可能會覺得很奇怪，為甚麼父母會告訴我這些事，但我認為他們很大方。當我知道前人是怎樣失敗的，我就可以避免自己再出現同樣的缺陷。這些年來我一直保持警惕，已經差不多撐到成年了。

不過，有一件令我擔憂的事情——最近我一直受偏頭痛困擾。開始時只是一個有顏色的光環，在我的視線裡轉來轉去，讓我看不到東西，然後就會帶來使人崩潰的痛楚。第一次是在學校發生，我還得哀求護士不要把我送回家；第二次是在一個過夜派對發生，那次我躲在毯子下面過了一整夜。

我不能永遠隱藏這件事，我的父母終有一天會發現。到了那天，四十八就會在等待著。

Girls Help Girls

I think it's really important that girls help girls.

Sure, that's obvious, but it's true. There's something special about the way that two drunk women can meet in a nightclub bathroom and, five minutes later, be the best of friends. It's an honest–to–God sisterhood. We share makeup, complement each other's style, add one another on social media. But, what's most important is that we protect each other.

There are some real creeps out there.

Take, for instance, the other night. I was freshening up in the ladies' room of this dive bar, when this one girl stumbled in, completely wasted. Apparently, Olivia was on a blind date that wasn't going so well. Poor thing got the impression that the guy expected her to put out, and wouldn't take "no" for an answer. Ugh, men. She tried to act calm, but I could tell that she was stalling to avoid returning to her table. Together, we chatted about life while I fixed her disarrayed hair and she sobered up.

After about 20 minutes, I decided it was finally time to get Olivia out of there. Locking my arm around hers, I marched us to a nearby bouncer and informed him of our situation. Under his watchful eye, I called Olivia a taxi. I noticed her date shooting me daggers from across the club, but he seemed

女孩互助互愛

我認為女孩互助互愛真的很重要。

是的，這不是甚麼新鮮事，但卻是真理。就像兩個喝醉的女子在夜店的廁所裡相遇，五分鐘後，就成了最好朋友，而且是真誠至上的好姐妹。我們分享化妝品，互補對方性格上的不足，交換彼此的社交媒體賬號。但是最重要的是我們互相保護著對方。

因為外面總會有些變態。

舉個例子，有一個晚上，我在一家酒吧的女廁梳洗時，一個完全喝醉了的女孩跌跌撞撞地走進來。顯然地，Olivia 剛見了陌生的網友，但結果不怎樣好。可憐的 Olivia 還讓對方誤以為她願意上床，怎麼拒絕他都聽不進去。唉，男人。她嘗試保持冷靜，但我看得出來，她正在拖延時間，她不想回到她的桌子。我們一起談人生的同時，我幫她整理好凌亂不堪的頭髮，她也清醒起來了。

大約二十分鐘後，我決定是時候帶走 Olivia。我扣著她的手臂，一起走到附近的保鏢身旁，並告訴他我們的情況。在他的看管下，我幫 Olivia 叫了一輛的士。我注意到她的約會對象在酒吧裡憤怒地望著我，但他似乎也明白了，並沒有接近我們。過了一會兒，戴好安全帶的 Olivia 安坐在的士裡面，

to get the message, and didn't approach us. Before long, Olivia was safely bundled into a cab and slurring gratitude at me through the window.

"You're such a doll...I love you so much babe..." she mumbled blearily, eyes half–shut, as the cab pulled away. I just smiled and reminded her to text me when she got home.

The saddest part of drunk–girl–conversations is never finding out what happened to the girl afterwards. Thankfully, that's not the case for Olivia and I.

I already know that her cab arrived at the docks shortly after 2am. I know that she was greeted by an assortment of men who, I'm sure, made her feel very welcome. I know that, as a virgin, she'll be sold for an exceedingly high price. She was a pretty one too– had an exotic look to her. I'm sure she'll fetch me and the boys a lot of money.

Once again, I'd like to reiterate how important it is that girls help girls.

I'm in the business of helping myself.

向車窗外的我表示感激之情。

「你簡直像個娃娃，寶貝我很愛你……」那輛的士一邊離開，雙眼半合的她一邊口齒不清地呢喃著。我只是報以微笑，提醒她回家時給我發短信。

最悲哀的是，醉酒女孩之間這些「意義深遠」的對話，從來不會幫助她們預知後來會發生甚麼事。幸運的是，這種情況不會出現在我和 Olivia 身上。

因為我早就知道那輛的士過了凌晨兩點就會到達碼頭。我知道，那裡會有一大堆男人招待她，我相信他們會令她覺得賓至如歸。我知道，作為一個處女，她可以賣得一個非常可觀的價錢。她很漂亮，而且有點異國風情，我相信她會為我和其他男孩帶來很多錢。

我想再一次重申，女孩互助互愛真的非常重要。

我現在就是在幫自己。

I Don't Have a Gay Son

A few months ago, my oldest son, Charlie, came out to me as a homosexual.

He sat his mother and I down in the living room and confessed everything to us; about how he had always felt attraction towards men, for his entire life. He even told us that he had a boyfriend who he wanted to introduce us to. Justine and I had always had our suspicions about Charlie, but we were still shocked by our son's revelation.

Suffice to say, Charlie is no longer a son of mine.

You see, every now and again, teenagers in our town get unnatural urges. We try to correct these impure desires early–teach kids right from wrong. If you don't nip these thoughts in the bud while they're still young, they'll manifest as behaviour in adolescence. We pull offending children up and tell them, again and again, from morning worship to Sunday school.

"Your ungodly impulses are a choice" we lecture. "You can choose Heaven or you can choose Hell. Which will it be?" For many youth, the threat of damnation is enough to set them on the right path. But there are those who cling to their perversions, convincing themselves that their lifestyle choice is the correct one.

我沒有同性戀兒子

幾個月前，我的大兒子 Charlie 出櫃了，跟我坦白說他是個同性戀者。

他讓我和他媽媽坐在客廳，向我們承認一切：說他一生以來其實一直都對男人有好感；他甚至告訴我們，他有個男朋友，想介紹給我們認識。Justine 和我一直懷疑 Charlie 是個同性戀者，但我們還是對兒子的坦白感到震驚。

我只想說，Charlie 不再是我的兒子。

你看看吧，每隔一陣子，我們城裡的青少年就會有違反自然的衝動。我們嘗試提早糾正這些不純潔的慾望，所以從小時候就要教育他們甚麼是對，甚麼是錯。如果你沒有把這些想法在萌芽時扼殺掉，那麼在青春期的時候就會表現出來。我們帶這些犯了錯的孩子到早晨崇拜和主日學校，一次又一次的勸教他們。

「你這些不虔誠的衝動其實是可以選擇的，」我們跟他講道理：「你可以選擇天堂，或者你可以選擇地獄。你會選哪個？」對於許多青年來說，詛咒的威脅已經足以使他們走回正確的道路，但還是會有些人堅持說服自己的生活方式就是正確的選擇。

If only we had beat it out of them. Maybe that could have saved Charlie.

I'll never understand what compels teens to commit such awful sin. Some say that it's the media, corrupting the minds of the youth. Others think that it's just the primal evil of humanity, inevitably seeping through. All I know for sure is that these teenagers go about defiling the Lord, and our town, remorselessly.

There are probably those out there who would call us intolerant. That's fine by us. We believe that there are some transgressions that simply shouldn't be tolerated, under any circumstances.

And we will never tolerate abduction, torture and murder.

No, I don't have a gay son. I don't have a gay son, because those twisted fucking bastards killed him.

如果我們可以從他們身上擊退這些衝動，也許可以拯救到 Charlie。

我永遠不會明白甚麼逼使青少年犯下這樣可怕的罪。有人會說是媒體腐化了年輕人的思想；又有人認為這只是人類的原始邪惡，無可避免地入侵著他們。但我可以肯定的是，這些青少年不知悔改地玷污著上帝、玷污著我們的城鎮。

可能有人會說我們沒有包容心，但對我們來說沒關係，因為我們相信，在任何情況下，都不應該容忍這些違法行為。

我們永遠不會容忍綁架、施酷刑和謀殺。

沒有，我沒有同性戀的兒子，我沒有同性戀的兒子，因為那些心理扭曲的混蛋已經把他殺死了。

Knock 'Em Dead, Kiddo

They told me 'knock 'em dead, kiddo'

You see, I'm a comedian. It's a gift I have to make people laugh. I've been told I'm fiendishly good at it. Enough that I could become famous if I really wanted to. But unlike some of my fellows, I have no grand ambitions to be on the big stage. No, I simply take whatever jobs I'm offered, and I go on stage and tell my jokes.

I've been all over the place. Comedy clubs. Small venues. Birthday parties for young children. I'm not picky about the jobs, provided they pay well enough. I'm simply told where to go, and boom! There I am, providing a rapid fire laugh a minute riot. The people can't stop laughing at my jokes.

Just last night, I was over at the Mad House in San Diego. Yeah, the one at Horton Plaza. Nice place. My focus tonight was on James Ritter, a heavyset middle aged gentleman. A regular from what I'd been told. Apparently he was a big shot in the area. Something about waste management. There was some rumors he was skimming off the top of his business. But what do I care, ain't none of my business, right? As long as he kept laughing, everything was good, and I'd get paid.

Now, I have to admit, I try and figure out what kind of jokes people like James like and tailor my set towards them. Get

小伙子，幹掉他

他們跟我說：「小伙子，幹掉他。」

我是個喜劇演員，逗人發笑是我的天賦。很多人都說我很擅長逗人發笑，如果我真的想要成名，我絕對可以勝任。但我不像伙伴們有著豪情壯志想登上大舞台，我不想。只要有工作給我我都會做，踏在舞台上講我的笑話，就是這麼簡單。

我走遍了很多地方：喜劇俱樂部、小場館、小孩生日聚會等等。我不挑剔，只要薪水高就可以了。別人請我去哪裡，我就在哪裡出現！我快速地投下了「笑足一分鐘」炸彈，觀眾聽完我的笑話都笑得停不下來。

就在昨天晚上，我獲邀到聖地亞哥的瘋狂屋喜劇俱樂部。是的，在 Horton 廣場的那個，那是個好地方。我將今晚的焦點放在 James Ritter 身上，他是個魁梧的中年紳士，跟我平常接到的任務差不多。顯然他是該區的大人物，好像是做廢物管理之類的。有謠言說他虧空公款，但我為啥要管他？那不關我的事，對吧？只要他有笑，我就有薪水，那就最好了。

我必須承認，我試著弄清楚像 James 這種人會喜歡甚麼類型的笑話，然後為他度身訂造可以惹他發笑的笑話。只要逗得他們哈哈大笑，其他人就會跟著一起笑。而今晚就做到

them laughing, and everyone else laughs right along. And it was working tonight. I had the audience in stitches! James was the best though. He laughed at every single joke and line I gave him. Seriously, he tried to stop laughing several times, but he couldn't find it in him to keep himself from laughing. Of course, I was going through joke to joke faster than a speed eater through hot dogs. I wasn't going to give him time to catch his breath.

But it was when I told my best and last line of the evening, when I focused all my comedic ability completely on him. The moment I finished the delivery, James gave what must have been the best bout of belly laughter he probably ever had for a few seconds, before he fell over onto the floor, dead as a door–nail. The doctors would later said he'd died from asphyxiation. He'd literally laughed himself to death. And as I watched on as the audience reacted in horror and calls to get an ambulance, I looked at the smile plastered across his face. It wasn't a bad way to go, all things considered. And I was going to get thirty grand for this one.

You see, I told you I have a gift to make people laugh. I'm fiendishly good at it. And the Mob in Los Angeles wanted James rubbed out. So they told me 'knock 'em dead, kiddo'

And that's just what I did.

了，我逗得觀眾捧腹大笑！James 是當中笑得最開心的一個，我說的每一個笑話和對白他都笑得樂不可支。我說真的，他有幾次都試著不要笑，但他不能控制自己不笑。當然啦，因為我拋出笑話的速度比大胃王鬥快吃熱狗還要快，我不會讓他有時間喘口氣。

在我說出了當晚最好和最後的一句對白時，我將所有的搞笑能力全部放在他身上，而在我說完的那一刻，James 發出了可能是他一直以來最開懷的大笑聲，幾秒之後就倒在地上，徹底的死去了。後來醫生說他死於窒息，所以他是真的「笑死」了。我看著觀眾驚恐的反應，他們都在慌忙地打電話叫救護車，再看看 James 臉上充滿著歡樂，這不算是太差的死法吧。所有的事情都在預算之內，然後我就會獲得三萬元報酬。

我就說吧，逗人發笑是我的天賦，我真的非常擅長講笑話呢。所以當洛杉磯的犯罪集團希望除去 James 的時候，他們吩咐我：「小伙子，幹掉他。」

那我就照辦啦。

Male or Female?

"Male."
"What colour do you want his eyes?"
"Blue, definitely blue."
"Okay, what about the hair?"

We looked at each other and nodded.

"Blonde."

The man smiled and we smiled back.

"Have you thought about a career?"
"Banker, something that makes a lot of money."
"Okie dokie. Girlfriend, boyfriend? I'm not judging."
"Girlfriend," we said in unison.
"Okay. Is there anything else?"
"We want him to be important."
"How important?"
"We want him to make a difference. Someone who is remembered for a long time."
"No problem...Okie dokie, this comes to around..."

He typed furiously on his keyboard.

"£3,200,000. Is that okay?"

男生還是女生？

「男生。」
「你想他的眼睛是甚麼顏色？」
「藍色，一定是藍色。」
「好的，那頭髮呢？」

我們望著對方，點了點頭。

「金色。」

那個男人笑了，我們也笑了。

「有沒有考慮要從事甚麼行業？」
「銀行家，可以賺很多錢的那種。」
「好的好的，女朋友還是男朋友？我不會有意見。」
「女朋友。」我們異口同聲地說。
「好的，還需要甚麼嗎？」
「我們希望他是個重要的人。」
「有多重要？」
「我們希望他有所作為，希望有人會記住他。」
「沒問題……好的，這樣就要差不多……」

他迅速敲打著鍵盤。

My head sank. My husband put his arm on my shoulder as I began to cry.

"We can't afford that," my husband said.
"You're not the first. Don't worry, we can work this out," the man said.
"All we have to do is give him some hardships."
"What do you mean?"
"Well, we can give him asthma; that will be £20,000 off the price. Diabetes is £30,000. Would that make a dent?"

We shook our heads.

"What's your budget?"
"Around £400,000."

The man checked his computer.

"Okay. But it will take a big sacrifice from you."
"We want the best for our son."
"You can make him an orphan. But you know what that means. As soon as we sign this..."
"No!"
"Otherwise you could die in a car crash when he is young. What blood type are you again?"
"AB positive."

「320 萬英鎊，可以嗎？」

我低下頭。我忍不住哭泣，丈夫就把手臂放在我的肩上。

「我們付不起。」我丈夫說。
「你不是第一個付不起錢的人，別擔心，我們可以解決這個問題，」男人說。
「我們只需給他一些困難就可以了。」
「那是甚麼意思？」
「嗯，我們可以給他哮喘，就可以減 2 萬英鎊，糖尿病就可以減 3 萬英鎊，這樣可以嗎？」

我們搖頭。

「你們的預算是多少？」
「約 40 萬英鎊。」

男人查看了一下電腦。

「好吧，但這樣你要作出很大的犧牲。」
「我們希望兒子可以有最好的東西。」
「你可以讓他成為一個孤兒，但你知道那是甚麼意思，一旦我們簽署了……」

"Good. That will work in your favour. We'll need a full body examination. Are you a smoker?"
"No."
"What about your husband. Is he happy to be involved too?"
"We need someone to take care of him. You can't have both of us."
"I'm sorry. We will need both of you if you want to go ahead; £3,200,000 is a lot of money to offset."

We looked at each other again and nodded.

"Yes, we are both happy to go ahead."
"Good. We promise, your son will be the person you want him to be. We'll send over the contracts in the next couple of days."
"Please, we want to see him graduate. One of us will need to be around until he gets on his feet."

"I understand your concerns. Mrs Williams, as you are AB positive, you would need to be harvested before he's ten. But Mr Williams we can afford to wait until your son is twenty. I know this is an important decision, so you don't need to make it now, take your time, think it over. If you want to go ahead, we can get the ball rolling and send the doctors over to evaluate your organs."

「不要！」
「不要的話，那在他年輕的時候，你就會遇上車禍身亡，你是甚麼血型來著？」
「AB 正型。」
「很好，這將會對你有利。那你們需要全身檢查，你吸煙嗎？」
「不吸。」
「你的丈夫怎麼樣，他也樂意參與嗎？」
「他需要有人照顧，你不能兩個人都要。」
「很抱歉，320 萬英鎊可不是個小數目，如果想繼續進行，就需要你們兩個人一起合作。」

我們再次望著對方，然後點點頭。

「是的，我們都很樂意繼續進行。」
「好的，我們承諾，你的兒子將會是你想要的模樣，在接下來的幾天內我們就會把合同寄給你們。」
「拜託，我們想看到他畢業，他需要我們其中一人在他身邊，直到他獨立為止。」

「Williams 太太，我明白你的疑慮，但因為你是 AB 正型，所以在他十歲前就要把你帶走，但 Williams 先生就可以等到兒子二十歲才被帶走。我知道這是一個重要的決定，所以

My husband looked at me anxiously. We wanted the best for our child and I would do anything to make sure he had the best start in life.

你不需要現在下決定，你可以仔細想清楚再決定。如果你想繼續下去，我們可以開始行動，派醫生去評估你的器官。」

丈夫焦急地望著我，但我們希望孩子可以有最好的東西，只要他的生活可以有個最好的開始，我願意為他做任何事情。

My Baby

I had a child. She was perfect. Blue eyes, a tuft of brown hair, tiny fingers and a button nose. And she was taken away from me. Torn from my arms by some monster.

My... precious, precious baby didn't cry.

I screamed with all my fury and anger at the cruel being, and it howled and wailed back at me. Like the savage it was, it tried to gather up the pieces of my baby. My beautiful baby... now bloody and dead.

I ran, for instinct told me if I wanted to live, I must run. I wallow in my grief for sometime, I don't know for how long until I see it.

A pretty little carriage in the park. With my new precious baby in it.

With outstretched claws I snatched it up protectively. My baby is so perfect. Chocolate brown eyes and wisps of black hair. I hug him tightly until I heard his cute little bones break and shatter and his eyes bulge out ever so slightly.

我的寶貝

我有個孩子，她那藍色的眼睛、棕色的頭髮，還有嬌小的手指和鼻子都使她很完美。但她被搶走了，有怪獸從我的懷抱裡把她搶走了。

我那珍而重之的寶貝並沒有哭。

我將所有怒氣化成咆哮，對著那殘暴的生物大叫大喊，然後牠也對我回喊並哀號著。牠像個原始人般，收集起我那被撕成了碎片的寶寶。我那美麗的寶貝……現在已變得血淋淋、奄奄一息。

我拔腿就跑，本能告訴我如果我想活下來就一定要跑。我有好一陣子只顧沉溺在悲痛裡。不知道過了多久之後，我看見了它。

一輛精緻的嬰兒車泊了在公園，還有我那新的珍貴小寶貝在裡面。

我伸出爪子把嬰兒車搶過來，保護著它。我的寶寶有著像巧克力的棕色眼睛和幾綹柔軟的黑色頭髮，真是太完美了。我用力地抱著他，直到聽到他可愛小骨頭破裂的聲音、看到他的眼睛微微凸出來為止。

Imagine my horror when I see another creature rushing at me, screaming and howling that familiar phrase.

"My son! My baby!"

God is so cruel to me. Why does this happen every time?

想像一下我看到的場景有多恐怖吧，另一隻尖叫著的生物向我衝過來，怒吼著那熟悉的語句：「兒子！我的寶貝！」

上帝對我真殘忍，為何每次都是這樣？

Never Trust a Man

I have always lived in this house. It's not very big, but it's home. This little house is where my children are, where we worship God together and wait for him to take us into his eternal home. I love the decor, the furniture, the wallpaper – all except for the green room. That's where the stairs up are, and I just generally avoid the place.

Once every two weeks, though, I have to go in. I must blindfold myself, take the stairs up into the bright room, hold my shaking hands out and hope it's her there, not him. It's a fifty/fifty shot, really. If he's there, I subjected to whatever horrific games he wants to play – my body doesn't belong to me anymore, I separate myself from it, and let him have his way. If it's her, I get a large crate of foods and drinks to take down to my house, to share with my four children. I can only tell who it is behind the blindfold by their voices. They both greet me, almost always the same way. If I hear his gruff, "There's my girl," I know I'm in for it. If I hear her melodiously melancholy, "Hello, dear," I know I'm safe.

The last time I went up, a week and a half ago, she greeted me in her classic way. I smiled to her, hoping she could tell I meant it despite not being able to see my eyes. But, when she handed me the box, she grabbed my wrist and whispered, "In the bottom of the box is a bottle. In that bottle are pills. If you ever hear someone else, if they ever come for us, you

不要相信男人

我一直住在這所房子裡，雖然不是很大，但這就是我的家。我跟孩子一起住在這個小房子，我們在這裡一起敬拜上帝，等待他帶領我們進入祂永恆的家園。我喜歡這裡的裝飾、傢具、壁紙，只是不喜歡那間綠色房間，上樓的樓梯就在那裡，但我通常都會避開那個地方。

可是，每隔兩個星期，我都必須進去一次。我要自己蒙住眼睛，走上樓梯，進入那明亮的房間，伸出我不住顫抖的手，希望在那裡的是她，而不是他。遇到他們的機會真的是一半一半。如果在那裡的是他，我就要讓他玩任何他想玩的可怕遊戲……我的身體不再屬於我，我將自己與肉體分離，讓他自得其樂。如果在那裡的是她，她會給我一大堆食物和飲料，讓我拿回家和我四個孩子分享。我只能透過他們的聲音來判斷出現的會是誰。他們都會跟我打招呼，而且每次也是大同小異的。如果我聽到他粗啞地說著：「這樣才對嘛。」我就知道自己倒霉了；如果我聽到她憂傷地說著：「嗨，親愛的。」我就知道自己安全了。

一個半星期前，是我最後一次上去，她一如以往地迎接我。我對她微笑著，希望她即使無法看到我的眼睛，也能知道我的意思。但是，當她把箱子交給我的時候，她抓住我的手腕，低聲說道：「盒子底部有個瓶子，瓶子裡有藥丸，如果聽到別人的聲音，或是他們來找我們的話，你知道怎樣做

know what to do."

"Of course. I know." And I did know. I have to protect myself, I have to protect my children. I know what men are capable of, and if they come I will do whatever is necessary.

And thank God she gave me those pills. She must have known they were coming. I have pushed all the furniture I can against the door that leads from the green room into our den. I cuddle my children close, each of us taking our little red pills with a sip of what's left of our water. I kiss each of my precious babies, my little joys, as the pounding on the door grows louder and my head starts to swim.

A man shouts from the other side, "Open up! This is the police. Please remain calm. We have Howard and Betsy Turner in custody. We're here to help you. Take you outside! You're safe now..."

I can feel everything getting old, my children have stopped moving, stopped crying. We must be close to God's big house now. I'm so glad the woman gave us those pills, kept us safe. I don't know what the police is, or who Howard and Betsy are, but I do know one thing – never trust a man.

吧。」

「我當然知道。」我真的知道，我必須保護自己，我必須保護我的孩子。我知道男人的本領，如果他們來了，我會採取一切必要措施。

我很感激她把這些藥給了我，我想她一定是知道他們要來了。我盡力把所有我能推得動的傢具都推到了那個連接著綠色房間和我們小房子的門口。我摟住我的孩子，我們每個人都喝了一口僅餘的水，把紅色小藥片吞下。門上砰砰作響，我的腦袋也開始亂轉，但我還是逐一親著曾經為我帶來快樂的心肝寶貝。

有個男人從另一邊喊道：「開門！我們是警察，請保持冷靜，我們已經扣押了 Howard Turner 和 Betsy Turner，我們是來幫你，帶你出去的！你們現在安全了……」

我可以感覺到一切開始衰老，我的孩子沒有再動、沒有再哭了。我們現在一定是離上帝的大房子很近了。我很感激那個女人給了我們那些藥，保衛了我們的安全。我不知道甚麼是警察，也不知道誰是Howard和Betsy，但我知道一件事——永遠不要相信男人。

Nightlight

There's a bad man in the house.

I wish I was asleep now. On the bed, snuggling into the covers with my doll while basking in the safety of the Disney themed nightlight in the corner of the room. But there was a scream, a thud, a yell, doors slamming and feet pounding.

I'm hiding now. I'm scared now. I want the bad man to go away. He can't find me under the bed. I'm not going to cry, I'm not a baby. I clutch my doll and wait. I see feet belonging to the bad man from where I was. He's pacing, yelling, knocking things over.

I want him to go away. But he's starting to kneel now, he's going to look under the bed. I finally whimper. I don't want the bad man to take me away. I don't want to die.

The bad man makes eye contact with me. He scared me so badly, that I accidentally break his daughter's neck.

小夜燈

房子裡有壞人。

我真希望我現在是睡著的。我躺在床上，抱著我的娃娃依偎在被窩裡，同時享受著放在房間角落的迪士尼主題小夜燈，它的光讓我覺得很安心。

但我聽見了尖叫聲、「轟」一聲、大叫聲、門的「砰砰」聲和雜亂的腳步聲。

我現在躲了起來，我很害怕。我想壞人快點離開。我躲在床下，他找不到我。我是不會哭的，我不是個孩子。我緊握著我的娃娃，然後等待。我從床下看到那屬於壞人的腳。他在踱步、大叫、把東西打翻。

我想他離開。但他現在開始跪下了，他要來看床下了。我終於嗚咽了，我不想讓壞人把我帶走。我不想死。

那壞人跟我的眼睛對上了。他嚇得我很慘，所以我不小心把他女兒的脖子弄斷了。

At the Corner of My Room

He always has a grin in his face, but it's a bloody grin, a flesh wound from ear to ear. And it always seemed freshly cut, as if someone had stabbed the corners of his mouth just minutes earlier. He had no hair, and more disturbingly, no eyes. It wasn't just empty sockets though, there was just no eyes there, as if it wasn't even human. Just straight, hard skin where the eyes are supposed to be. He is tall as well, probably about 6' 4" and very pale, white as the exposed bone of a broken leg. His thin arms end in very long, pointy fingers with dark nails, not painted, rotten. He dresses in dirty grey rags and if you get close enough, you'll be able to listen to a faint, heavy breathing.

I was 6 years old when I first saw him. Woke up at night and there he was, at the corner of my room, long arms barely moving, the dirty white head facing me with no eyes to see. I yelled, my parents came running in. A monster, I said. There are no monsters, they told me. It was still there, but they couldn't see him. As time went on, they started thinking I was crazy, so I stopped talking about it. Years passed. He would go away sometimes, for a few days, maybe weeks, but sooner or later, wherever I was, he'd appear in the corner of the room, standing, watching. That went on for years, it's the only life I ever knew. The constant fear, the expectation for the day he'd finally do something, hurt me.

在我房間的角落

他臉上總是掛著笑容，但那是一個血淋淋的笑容：一道傷口從一邊耳朵伸延到另一邊耳朵。而且那傷口看起來總是像剛剛才受傷，好像在幾分鐘前才有人刺傷他的嘴角般。他沒有頭髮，更令人不安的是，他沒有眼睛。那個位置不是個沒有眼珠的凹槽，而根本不像是人類的樣子，而是有又平又硬的皮膚覆蓋著本來應是眼睛的地方。他很高，大概有6呎4吋，而且非常蒼白，白得像斷腿暴露出來的骨頭。他的手臂很幼，有著長而尖的手指，指甲很深色，但那不是畫上去的，而是因為腐爛掉而變黑。他穿著土灰色的爛布衣，如果你離他夠近，你可以聽到微弱而沉重的呼吸聲。

我在六歲那年第一次見到他。晚上醒來，見到他出現在我房間的角落，那長長的手臂勉強地擺動著，那骯髒的白頭朝向我，但他沒有眼睛可以望著我。我大聲尖叫，我的父母跑進來我房間。「有怪物。」我說。「不會有怪物的。」他們告訴我。他還在，但我父母看不見他。隨著時間流逝，我父母開始認為我發瘋了，所以我沒有再談起他。又再過了幾年，他有時會離開幾天甚至幾個星期，但遲早，無論我在哪裡，他都會出現在房間的角落，站在那裡，望著我。很多年以來一直也是這樣，我的生活就只有這樣。恐懼不斷籠罩著我，生怕有一天他會做些甚麼來傷害我。

But one day I discovered a local psychic in a newspaper ad. I went to see her and, as soon as I sat down to tell my problem, he appeared. I was scared, but… she saw it, she could see him as well. That was a first. So I asked her, I begged her to help me. How do I get rid of him? And she told me, she really did.

What you must do, she said, is tell people. Tell them how he looks. Describe it as best as you can, really make them visualize him. They'll imagine, and someone, someday, will get it right. Someone will come close enough, picture just the right appearance. That's what lures him in. Once he's inside your mind, he's inside your life. She told me that when someone picture him just right, eventually that person will enter a room and he will be waiting there, at the corner, with his bloody grin, and I will be free at last.

但有一天，我在報紙廣告中發現了一個當地的靈媒。我去了找她，當我一坐下，開始講述我的困擾時，他就出現了。我很害怕，但是……她也看到了，她也可以看到他。她是第一個見到他的人。所以我向她求助，我拜託她來幫幫我。我問她我要如何擺脫他？她告訴我解決方法，她真的告訴我了。

她說，你要做的，就是告訴人們。告訴他們他長得怎麼樣的，盡可能詳細地描述它，努力讓他們可以把他形象化。他們會開始想像，終有一天，他們會想像得到的。然後有人會靠得夠近，想像得恰到好處。那就是引誘他出現的方法。一旦他在你的腦海裡，他就會在你的生活出現。她告訴我，當有人把他描繪得恰到好處的時候，最終有個人會進入房間，他就會帶著那血淋淋的笑容在那邊等著，然後我就終於可以自由了。

Once More, from the Top

Once more on March 16th, 2017, at 5:13 AM, Sammy Rivers opened his eyes.

He inwardly sighed, waiting for the requisite 3 minutes and 10 seconds to pass before getting out of bed, like he always did. Never a second later or earlier.

Sammy could do his daily routine with his eyes closed by this point. Go to the bathroom, get himself showered and groomed. Get dressed, and make a quick breakfast of blueberry pancakes. They'd once been his favorite, through the first couple of iterations. But now the flavor held no joy. It was just more of the same, every time.

At 6:49, Sammy left his house, and started towards his work. He could see the nameless strangers as he walked past, all busy with their own routines. By this point, he knew all of their features by heart, but nothing about the people themselves. Sammy would have loved to talk to them. Maybe learn something new about these strangers. But that hadn't happened the first time he walked to work, and doing so this time would be a deviation. And as he had learned so long ago, deviations were not accepted.

從頭再來一次

2017 年 3 月 16 日上午 5 點 13 分，Sammy Rivers 再一次張開了眼睛。

他在內心嘆了口氣，一如以往，必須多等 3 分鐘 10 秒的時間才能下床。從來不會早一秒或遲一秒。

到了現在，Sammy 已經可以閉著眼處理日常程序：去洗手間，洗澡和打扮。穿好衣服，來個快速的藍莓煎餅早餐。藍莓煎餅曾是 Sammy 的最愛，不過只限於頭幾次的迭代。但現在對 Sammy 來說這個每次都是一樣的味道，已經由美味變得淡而無味。

6 點 49 分，Sammy 離開家門上班去。他走過那些叫不出名字的陌生人身旁，各自忙著自己的工作。到了現在，Sammy 對他們所有的特徵都瞭如指掌，但對他們的內在卻一竅不通。Sammy 很想跟他們說說話，這樣也許可以了解這些陌生人多一點。但是，他第一次上班沒有這樣做，如果今次這樣做就會出現誤差。正如他早已學會的，誤差是不被接受的。

At 7:15, he finally made it to his job over at Sweetwater High School, like he always did. There, he'd teach the students about America's contribution to World War II to students who had heard him teach it for... five hundred? Six hundred? Sammy wasn't quite sure anymore, and he was pretty sure if he'd asked his students, they wouldn't know either. There would be quiz, like always. And he already knew what each student would answer. Everyone knew the right answer was irrelevant, and getting it correct this time might get them noticed.

At 4:03 in the afternoon, when his work day had finally ended, Sammy started his trek back towards his house. Oh, he'd never reach it. Sammy knew that at 4:23, he'd be mugged for the money in his wallet, and shot in the head right after he gave it to him. Idly, Sammy wondered if they ever caught the man.

Sure enough, at 4:23, the mugger showed up. Sammy could see the dead look in his eyes as he approached. The same dead look he saw in everybody's eyes nowadays. Sammy wondered if the thief was just as tired of shooting him as he was of getting shot. But they both had to go through with it, like always. There had been one time where the robbery and murder did not take place, so many cycles ago. Neither of them had any desire to go through what had happened

7點15分，一如以往，他到達了Sweetwater中學，那是他工作的地方。在那裡，他會教導學生有關美國對第二次世界大戰的貢獻，那些學生已經聽他說過……五百？還是六百次？Sammy不太確定，但他可以肯定的是，就算問他的學生，他們也不會知道。一如以往，Sammy會派發測驗卷給學生。他已經知道每個學生會回答甚麼。每個人都知道正確答案已經不重要了，而且如果這次答對了可能會引起他們的注意。

下午4點03分， Sammy一天的工作終於結束了，他走著回家的路。哦，他永遠不會回到家，因為他知道自己將會在4點23分被搶劫，正當他拿出錢包裡的錢之際，就會被槍射中頭部。有時在做白日夢時，Sammy會想他們會不會有一天抓到這個男人。

果然，在4點23分，劫匪出現了。當劫匪向Sammy走近時，他看到劫匪那毫無生氣的眼神，那個現在每個人眼中都能看到的眼神。Sammy在想那個劫匪在射殺他時，會否像自己被射殺時一樣感到厭倦。但是，他們都一定要像以往一樣，繼續進行。曾經試過有一次，搶劫和謀殺都沒有發生，不過那是很多周期之前的事了。沒有人想去經歷後來發生的事，在第一次之後就沒有人再做過了。

afterwards. Nobody did after the first time.

As always, he was robbed. And as always, he was shot in the head. It always took him a few seconds to die. Just long enough to hear something whispering "Once more, from the top."

And once more on March 16th, 2017, at 5:13 AM, Sammy Rivers opened his eyes.

一如以往，他被搶劫了。然後一如以往，劫匪向他的頭部開了槍。然後總會花上幾秒鐘才會真正死去，這幾秒鐘剛好讓他聽到有人在他耳邊說：「從頭再來一次。」

2017 年 3 月 16 日上午 5 點 13 分，Sammy Rivers 又再一次張開了眼睛。

Schizophrenia with Severe Violent Tendencies

"Mr Johnston, it says here that you have schizophrenia with severe violent tendencies," the psychiatrist murmured checking his notes, his reading glasses resting on his nose. "Sharing with me won't reduce your prison sentence," he continued, "But it may go someway to clear your conscience, you understand?"

I nodded.

"So, where would you like to start?"
"The voices," I said, staring at the ceiling.
"Voices, hmmm; are they threatening?"
"Sometimes."
"Do they make you angry?"
"You could say that."
"Do you hear them now?"
"No."

The psychiatrist sighed, I winced at the cracking of his wicker chair as he sunk into it.

How much longer do I have with this criminal piece of shit?

"Around thirty–five minutes doc," I responded gritting my teeth.
Startled, he replied, "I'm sorry?"

有嚴重暴力傾向的精神分裂症患者

「Johnston 先生，這裡說你有精神分裂症，而且有嚴重暴力傾向。」戴著老花眼鏡的精神科醫生邊翻閱我的病歷邊呢喃著。「雖然跟我分享並不會減少你的刑期，」他繼續說：「但好歹也會使你良心好過一點，你明白了嗎？」

我點點頭。

「好吧，你想從哪裡開始？」
「那些聲音。」我望著天花說。
「聲音，唔……它們有威脅性嗎？」
「有時有。」
「它們會讓你很生氣嗎？」
「可以這樣說。」
「你現在有聽見它們的聲音嗎？」
「沒有。」

醫生嘆了口氣，沉沉的跌坐在藤椅。我聽見那些藤子斷裂的聲音，不禁皺起眉頭。

我還要對著這坨狗屎罪犯多久？

「大約三十五分鐘吧醫生。」我咬牙切齒地說。
他怔了一下，回答道：「你說甚麼？」

"You have to talk to *this criminal piece of shit* for thirty–five, hang on, thirty–four more minutes."
"I... I... don't understand?"

Can he hear my thoughts?

"Yes I can."
"Oh, uh, how unique. Can you hear everything I am thinking about, son?"
"Pretty much."
"Oh my God," he said panicking, "I... I... think you should leave!"
"But what about my conscience?" I said in a sarcastic tone.

He scrambled to his feet and ran to the door; he opened it and closed his eyes tight, pointing the way to my exit, "Please leave!"

I pushed myself off the couch and made my way to the door.

Don't think about your daughter, don't think about what you do to her.

I stopped and turned, "I'm sorry? What do you do to your daughter?" I grimaced, and put my hands around his neck, "You sick fuck!"

「你還要對著*這坨狗屎罪犯*，三十五，不對，三十四分鐘。」
「我不懂你的意思。」

他聽到我在想甚麼嗎？

「是的，我聽到。」
「噢，呃，很厲害啊。你聽到我所想的一切嗎？」
「幾乎吧。」
「我的天啊，」他驚慌地說：「我……我想你應該要離開了！」
「那我的良心怎麼辦？」我用諷刺的語調問道。

他奮然站起來跑到門前，然後打開門，緊閉著眼睛，指著出口方向說道：「請你離開！」

我從沙發站起來走向門口。

不要想起你的女兒，不要想起你對她做過甚麼。

我停下腳步轉身說：「你說甚麼？你對你的女兒做了甚麼？」
我齜牙咧嘴地用雙手圍著他的脖子叫道：「你這個變態！」

Simple Thrills

The fortune teller was never wrong. If you had the money and the guts, she could show you the last moments right before you died. I knew people who had been to her and told of what they had seen. I've seen her predictions come true on several occasions.

It didn't take too much thought before I decided to see her myself. I'm naturally curious. The vision she showed me was stunning. As I gazed into her crystal ball, the world faded and I was walking down the back road near my house, in the dark. The crickets chirped in the shadows. The crisp, cold air nipped at my nose. And then darkness. I didn't see how I died. The fortune teller said we didn't always see our deaths, sometimes just the moments before. The ball, she said, showed us only what we needed to see.

That vision changed my life. It's easy to take risks when you know they aren't risky. That back road I'm supposed to die on? It's not the only way to get to my house. All I had to do is avoid it and I didn't have to worry about a thing. I could go bungie jumping or sky diving or swim with sharks without worry of lasting harm. I was able–bodied in my vision so I knew nothing bad could happen to me. And the thrills were wonderful. But of course, thrills quickly stop becoming thrills when you take away the danger.

單純的刺激

算命師從來都不會出錯的，如果你有錢又有勇氣，你就可以請她讓你看看自己死前的最後一刻。我知道曾經去過找她的人，都看到了他們死前的畫面。我看過她的預言有幾次真的成真了。

我沒有想太多，就決定了要見她，我只是出於好奇。她向我展示的畫面實在是目不暇給。當我注視著她的水晶球時，我看見整個世界褪色了，而我自己就在黑暗中走在我家附近的小徑上。蟋蟀沒在陰影裡啁啾著，乾燥的冷空氣颼進我的鼻子裡。然後一片黑暗。我沒看到我是怎樣死的。算命師說，不是每次也會看到我們的死亡，有時只會看到死前一刻。她說，水晶球只會顯示我們需要看到的東西。

那個畫面改變了我的生活。當你知道那些事物沒有風險的時候，你就會願意冒險。我會死在那條小徑上？那不是我回家的唯一方法，所以只要我不走那條路，我就不必擔心。我可以去笨豬跳、跳傘、與鯊魚一起游泳，也不用擔心會受傷。在畫面中的我很健壯，所以我知道不會有甚麼壞事在我身上發生。那些驚險刺激的體驗很棒。但當然，當驚險的事情失去了危機感的時候就不再刺激了。

Don't get me wrong: I still love the extreme sports and the risky adventures. I ran with the bulls last month. I had a blast. But lately I've taken to a different type of thrill. Once a month, after the sun goes down, I put on my coat and I take a walk, right down the road. Yeah, that road.

As I walk down that road, hear the crickets chirp, feel the cold wind blowing through my hair, I find myself undergoing a transformation. The solid, fearless foundation I have in the face of cliffs and sharks and charging bulls starts to fracture and crumble with every step I take. As I approach the spot where the fortune teller's vision goes black, I feel my chest tighten. The hairs on the back of my neck stand on end. The sound of the crickets gives way to the thrum of blood as my heart frantically pumps. I shudder and then close my eyes, waiting, wondering if this is the moment I die. I continue to walk, eyes closed, and brace for the icy sting of a blade or the fangs of some unknown beast. Fear floods my mind and when I can take it no longer, I open my eyes again, never knowing whether I'll see the end of my street or the grinning visage of Death.

And for that glorious moment in time, I feel truly alive.

不要誤會，我還是很喜歡極限運動和危險的活動。就像是上個月，我和一群公牛一起跑步，我非常樂在其中。但是最近我決定要挑戰另一種刺激。每個月我都會挑一天，在太陽落下之後，穿起外套，走在小徑上。是的，就是那條小徑。

當我走在那條小徑時，我聽見蟋蟀唧唧作響，感覺到寒風拂過我的頭髮，我覺得自己好像要蛻變一樣。那些在我面對懸崖、鯊魚、和猛衝的公牛時，訓練出堅實無畏的基礎，現在卻隨著我的每一步開始破裂、剝落。當我去到在算命師那邊看到畫面變黑的那個地方，我感到有股壓迫感壓在胸膛，使我頸背的毛髮都豎了起來。心臟瘋狂跳動，血液流動的低鳴，蓋過了蟋蟀的叫聲。我發著抖，然後閉上眼睛，等待著，想著此刻是否要死掉了。我閉著眼繼續走著，準備被刀劍，或是被未知野獸殺死。恐懼淹蓋了我的腦海，當我不能再忍受的時候，我再次睜開眼睛，迎接著不知道會是街道的盡頭還是死亡對著我咧嘴而笑的光景。

而在那個光輝的時刻，我才真真正正的感到自己正在活著。

The Judgment of Cupid

"Do you have anything to say before sentence is carried out?" I looked towards my wife, hoping to find any trace of mercy in her face. "I'm sorry. I didn't mean to..."
But her face hardened. Whatever love had once been there was now gone. "You knew what you did."

That's all she said before turning her back to me, a finality in the statement.

I looked back to the person before me, his bow in hand. "Please, I wasn't aware how much it would hurt her."

Cupid just looked down at me with those cold, pitiless eyes. The look I have received from everyone ever since he came to punish me for my crime. But he was no happy baby with a toy arrow. No, this was a rugged and strong man. A full head of hair and a manly beard adorned his face. "The fact that you abandoned the love of your life to fornicate with your boss was detestable enough. Was getting a promotion really worth throwing away the future you could have had?"

I tried to speak, but the words died in my throat. I had told my boss that I would do whatever it took to get promoted, and she made the suggestion. There was no hesitation on either of our parts at all. A nice dinner and a night of lovemaking was simply the cost to be promoted.

邱比特的審判

「在行刑之前，你有話要說嗎？」

我看著我的妻子，盼望著在她臉上會找到一絲憐憫的痕跡。

「對不起，我不是想……」

但她面如死灰，我們的愛已經不復從前了。「你應該很清楚自己做了甚麼。」

她再沒有多說一句，轉身背對著我，成為了證詞的終結。

我回頭看著我身邊拿著弓的那個人：「求求你，我不知道會對她造成這麼深的傷害。」

邱比特只用他那雙冷酷無情的眼睛低頭看著我。自從邱比特要下來懲罰我之後，每個人都以這個模樣看著我。他絕對不是個拿起玩具箭頭的可愛寶寶。不是的，他是個粗獷又強壯的男人，有著豐厚的頭髮，留著雄赳赳的鬍子。「你放棄了你人生中的所愛，來跟老闆通姦，這件事實在是令人作嘔。升職真的那麼重要嗎？將你可能有的未來通通拋諸腦後，值得嗎？」

我欲言又止。我跟老闆說過，為了升職我願意做任何事情，然後她提出了這個建議。我們雙方也毫不猶豫，只需要一頓美好的晚餐和一個做愛的晚上，就可以換來升職的機會了。

"But to do so on my day made your crime even worse! A day for lovers to stroke the flames of passion and embrace what it was that brought them together in the first place. To cherish what your future together. And what makes the whole thing even worse is that it wasn't even for passion or a rival love! You couldn't even manage lust! No, you traded your love and faithfulness for business." That last word came out in disgust. I felt his eyes boring into my very soul. "So when your wife's anguished cries reached my ears, I came down from Olympus for the first time in a long while to render judgment on your wretched soul."

Cupid drew back his bow. I could see the taut strings, wanting to release the nocked arrow that was aimed directly at my heart. "You will not die when my arrow strikes you. Instead, you will live with the four loves denied to you for the rest of your days. You will never again feel the familial bonds of Storge, the friendship of Philia, the pleasures of Eros, or the closeness of Agape. You will be unloved, in all sense of the word, forever. This is my judgment for your crimes, and it is absolute."

I tried to cry out. To beg some more. To say I was sorry. But the only thing that came out were the tears in my eyes as the Olympian let loose his arrow, completing the sentence that no mortal could deny.

「但你竟然選擇了在我的大日子這樣做，使你的罪惡更嚴重！在那一天戀人會擦出激情花火，並感恩二人能在一起原來有多難能可貴，然後一起珍惜未來。你知道甚麼使整件事情更糟糕嗎？是這件事根本不存在任何激情或愛意！你根本不能控制性慾！不，你是用愛和忠誠來作生意交易。」他嫌惡地説著最後一句話。我彷彿感到他的眼睛看盡了我的靈魂。「所以當你妻子那撕心裂肺的哭泣聲傳入我的耳朵時，使我長期以來第一次從天堂下來，對你的猥褻靈魂作出審判。」

邱比特拉了弓，我看到那些繃緊的弦線，渴望著把那直接瞄准我心臟的箭頭發射出來。

「當我的箭擊中你時，你不會死亡。相反，你的餘生將不會再被愛。你永遠不會再感受到由家庭、友誼、激情和親密所帶來的愉悦。你永遠不會再有人愛你。這是我對你所犯罪行的審判，不會有任何更改。」

我很想大聲呼喊，多乞求他幾次，説我很抱歉。但我只能流著眼淚，望著邱比特射出了他的箭，完成他那沒有任何凡人能反抗的判刑。

The Regrets of a Time Traveler

I am a time traveler. Or I mean I was.

I was able to travel through time to whenever I wanted. I was a scientist with a great mind, I think, being the only person in my generation to discover time travel. I say I think because I don't remember my past. The earliest memory I could recall was entering euphoria. My vision sparked colors I've never seen before, my body dissipated into millions of tiny particles, and suddenly, I'm in another dimension of time. Amazing, right? The thing is, whenever I travel time, through that tunnel that propels all of the particles and atoms that are a part of me, I lose a portion of my memory, somewhere in that jumble of hyperspace. After my first time travel, I forgot everything.

Ever since then, I've taken caution to how I time travel and how often I do it. I've chosen to limit my abilities to inhibit the possibility of forgetting something important. I've forgotten a multitude of things, some smaller than others.

Around a year ago, I forgot the color of my hair, only to remember immediately upon seeing my reflection in the mirror. But it's been worse. Not too long ago, I forgot how to breathe on my own. It wasn't until I passed out that my innate human response was to breathe subconsciously.

時空旅人的遺憾

我是個時空旅人，或者説我曾經是。

我以前可以隨時穿梭時空，我想我曾經是個有著偉大思想的科學家吧，因為我是這一代唯一一個發現時空旅行的人。我説「我想」是因為我不記得我的過去。我能回想起最早的記憶是我進入了亢奮狀態，它引發了我的視覺，使我看見了以前從未見過的顏色，我的身體消散在數百萬的微小顆粒之中，突然之間，我就已經身處另一個時間維度。很厲害吧？但是，每當我穿梭時空，通過那條隧道的時候，會推動我身體的所有粒子和原子，都會使我失去一部分的記憶，遺失在那片混亂超時空的某個地方。在我第一次穿梭時空之後，我失憶了。

從那次之後，無論是穿梭時空的方法或者多久才穿梭一次，我都會謹慎處理。我選擇限制我的能力，希望可以減少遺忘重要事物的可能性。我忘記了許多東西，也有些不太重要的事。

大約一年前，我忘記了我的頭髮的顏色，只有在鏡子裡看到鏡像時才立刻記得。但更糟糕的是，不久以前，我忘了如何呼吸，直到我昏倒了，我的本能才替我潛意識地呼吸。

In the end, It was my curiosity that screwed me over.

On June 18, 9214, scientists, with the assistance of advanced supercomputers developed a prototype, an invention capable of previewing possible occurrences of forthcoming events. The minds of this millennium were able to see the freaking future. The display, provided by code and text, made expert computer programmers look like toddlers playing with C++. Nevertheless, they read it, and with time, created illustrations of the future. It ran for 3 years, producing accurate images of the upcoming events. But in 9217, it stopped working. The end date produced an incoherent image, a blurry picture of an unfocused earth. Scientists collaborated and thought this would be the end of existence, the complete opposite of the big bang. Religious wackos thought it was the apocalypse and the end of God himself. I thought that I could find the truth.

In the machines, I saw the days before the end, a hazy picture of a dark and decaying planet. Being a time traveler, I knew I could find out what would end us all. If I knew, I could come back and warn everyone of what would happen or maybe even save us all. That's why I decided to go there, to find out what the hell happens and go down in the books.

And I did. Boy, do I regret it.

到頭來，我的好奇心害死了自己。

9214年6月18日，科學家在超級電腦的協助下，研發了一個原型，這個發明可以預覽到即將發生事件不同的可能性，這個匯集千年智慧的機器可以看到未來。由代碼和文本組成的介面，使專業的電腦程式員看起來像小孩子在玩程式設計語言C++般。然而，他們嘗試理解它，過了好一段時間，機器就製造了未來的插圖。它為這三年來即將發生的事件提供了準確的影像。但到了9217年，它不再運作了，它停住的那一天，出現了一張不連貫的影像，一張模糊、失焦的地球畫面。科學家們相互合作，認為這將是與大爆炸完全相反的存在——結束；那些信教的怪胎就認為那是啟示和上帝自己本身的終結。我以為我可以找到真相。

在機器裡，我看到末日前的日子，一個黑暗、正在腐化星球的朦朧畫面。作為一個時空旅人，我知道我可以找到導致我們終結的原因。我知道了後就我可以回來，警告每個人之後會發生甚麼事，甚至可能救到所有人。所以我決定去那裡，看看發生了甚麼事，並寫在書中流傳下去。

我去了，但是，我很後悔。

I was trembling, my bowels loosened, my stomach turned. I was terrified.

Not because the tall man with the inhuman grin on his face was walking towards me.

Not because the screams that filled my ears did not sound like humans.

Not because I had just found hell on earth.

But because I forgot how to time travel.

我在發抖，我的腸子攪動著，胃子翻滾著……我嚇壞了。

並非因為那個帶著不像人類笑容的高大男人正在走近我。
不是因為充斥著我耳朵的尖叫聲不像是由人類發出的。

也不因為我在地球發現了地獄。

而是因為，我忘記了怎樣穿梭時空。

Bank Robbery

"Shut up and put it in the bag! Now!"

I can hear Shaun all the way from the lobby, shouting down the poor counter girl as she tries to hold onto some semblance of composure. I feel bad, but it's gotta be done.

I look at the terrified people in the lobby and keep my shotgun trained on them. I've done this at least a dozen times and every time I'm racked with guilt. The muffled sobbing always kills me. But it's better than having Shaun's job. I much prefer crowd control to actual robbery.

I lean back into the hallway and yell out.
"Shaun, time's almost up!"
"Don't rush me!" he roars. I really hope he can control himself in there. If not, the police will be the least of our problems.

As I turn back, I nearly have my head knocked off. One of the hostages decided to be brave. I jump back, dodging a wild punch and then smash the butt of my shotgun right into his nose. He crumples and the rest of the hostages start to scream. I can barely hear them though. The attack keyed me up and I try to bring myself back down. I take a few long, controlled breaths and feel myself come back to my senses. It was close. If I hadn't laid that guy out as quickly as I did, the

銀行劫案

「閉嘴！把它放進袋裡！快！」

我聽見 Shaun 在大堂裡向那個嘗試保持冷靜、可憐的櫃檯女孩叫嚷著。我覺得很糟糕，但沒辦法，我們必須這樣做。

我看著大堂裡那些被嚇壞的人，然後用霰彈槍指著他們。雖然這回事我已經幹過至少已經十幾次，但每次我都會被內疚感折磨。那些抑壓著的飲泣聲總是要了我的命。但這還是比 Shaun 的工作好一些。我會寧願負責維持人質秩序，也不想真的去搶劫。

我靠著走廊向著大堂叫道：「Shaun，時間差不多了！」
「別催我！」他吼道。我真的希望他能控制到自己。否則，我們的難題已經夠多了，更不用說警察那邊。

當我把頭轉回來的時候，我的頭差點沒了。其中一個人質決定要表現他的勇敢。我退後，躲了一拳，然後把霰彈槍的槍托猛塞進他鼻子裡。他被我打垮了，其他人質開始尖叫，不過我都不太能聽到他們的聲音。這次受襲令我變得繃緊，我嘗試讓自己恢復原狀。我深呼吸了幾下，感覺到自己的狀態恢復了。他剛剛差點就成功了，如果我收拾那傢伙的動作再慢一點，這晚的行動就會化為烏有了。我向著尖叫的人群怒吼，叫他們閉嘴，然後用霰彈槍掃過他們頭部的位置。他

night would have gone sideways. I yell at the screaming crowd to shut up and wave my shotgun over their heads. They clam up.

A few more moments and I see Shaun running down the hallway, his pillowcase bulging with the loot. I waste no time in barreling out the door and into the night, Shaun right behind me.

We run for several blocks and turn into an alley where our van waits for us. I throw the back doors open as Shaun hops into the driver's seat and starts the engine. A few minutes and we're headed out of town.

"How'd we do?" I rasp, pulling off my ski mask.
"Not bad" Shaun says. "We should be good for about a month."

I reach into the pillowcase and pull out the glorious dark red pouch. I rip it open and pour the contents into my mouth. I gag slightly as the coppery taste coats my tongue.

"I hate O negative," I groan. "Please tell me there's some B positive in here."
"I got what I could get," Shaun replies. "But save some of that O negative for me."

們馬上靜下來了。

再過了一會兒，我看到 Shaun 沿著走廊跑過來，手上拿著那個裝著戰利品的枕頭套。我爭分奪秒地奔向門口，逃離這裡，而 Shaun 就跟在我後面。

我們跑了幾個街區，然後拐進了一條胡同，我們把貨車泊了在這裡。我打開後門，Shaun 跳進駕駛座，啟動引擎。幾分鐘後，我們就朝城外方向逃去了。

「我們做得怎麼樣？」我邊尖聲地問，邊脫著我的滑雪面罩。
「不錯，」Shaun 說：「這裡應該可以撐到一個月。」

我把手伸進枕頭套，拿出一個亮麗的深紅色小袋。我撕開它，然後把裡面的東西倒進嘴裡。我有點作嘔，因為有股銅鏽味包覆著我的舌頭。

「我討厭 O 負，」我埋怨道：「拜託這些包裡面一定要有 B 正。」
「我已經盡力了，」Shaun 回答：「留點 O 負給我。」

I shudder a little and take a few more deep gulps. I can feel the tension, fury, and consuming hunger melt away as I drink.

Sometimes I wonder if it's worth the effort stealing this stuff when we could just go out and drain a few runaways in the middle of the night. But I just can't bring myself to do it. So knocking over blood banks it is. A guy's gotta have a little moral grounding.

我打了個哆嗦，然後又再喝了幾大口。我一邊喝，一邊感受到所有緊張、憤怒和飢餓感全部一掃而空。

有時候，我會想既然可以半夜出門使那些離家出走的傢伙變得乾巴巴，那這樣去偷東西值不值得呢？但我不准自己這樣做，所以就去「血液銀行」搗亂了。男子漢要應該有點道德原則才對。

Together for a Short While

"You know you can't keep doing this, right?"
I look up to the love of my life, my head currently laying on his lap. "I know, but it's Valentine's Day! You know, the time when lovers are supposed to be together?"
A slight chuckle escapes my boyfriend's lips. "Funny. Last time I looked, Valentine's Day was the day you were supposed to buy cheap chocolates and dead roses because otherwise you were an awful person who didn't truly love your girl."

I held back a giggle myself, as I imagined him trying to buy chocolates and roses. That would probably turn a few heads. Though that might ruin his reputation just a tiny bit. "I don't need those things. I just want you." Sure, it was a cheesy and cliché thing to say. But it was also true. I wasn't someone who cared about simple baubles.
I could feel my lover's fingers caress my head. "I know. It frustrates me too, that we can only be together for a short while. Let me guess, was it Tina this time? "
I sighed. "Yeah, she was just going on and on about how her boyfriends are giving her all these expensive gifts..."
"Wait, boyfriends? Plural?"
"Yeah, she's stringing four different men along. I don't think she actually loves any of them. But it got me jealous. She gets to spend Valentine's day with her boy–toys, and..." I could feel a bony finger rest upon my mouth, silencing my frustrations. He looks into my eyes, and I can feel myself melt in his gaze.

短暫的相聚

「你知道不可以繼續這樣做，對吧？」
我躺在他的腿上，仰望著我一生的最愛。「我知道，但今天是情人節嘛！今天是個戀人要待在一起的日子嘛！」
男朋友忍不住笑了：「真有趣，情人節應該是人們買廉價巧克力和凋謝玫瑰的日子，因為如果不這樣做就代表他不是真正愛他的女朋友。」

我邊想像他試著買巧克力和玫瑰給我的樣子，邊忍著笑。那可能會有一些人回頭看他吧，儘管這樣做會輕微破壞他的聲譽。「我不需要那些東西，我只想要你。」是的，這聽起來像是俗氣又陳詞濫調的對白。但我是真的這樣想，我不是那種喜歡那些小玩意的人。
我感覺到愛人的手指撫摸著我的頭。「我知道，我們能在一起的時間很短，這也使我很失望。讓我猜猜看，這次是 Tina 嗎？」

我嘆了口氣：「是的，她滔滔不絕地說她那些男朋友送她昂貴的禮物……」
「等一下，那些男朋友？複數？」
「是的，她正在跟四個不同的男人交往。我不認為她有真心愛他們任何一個，但我很妒忌她，因為她可以和她的男孩們一起度過情人節，而且……」我感覺到一根瘦骨嶙峋的手指放在我的唇上，止住了我的沮喪。他看著我的眼睛，我感覺

"Trust me, I understand how you feel, But I wouldn't be too jealous of her. I've seen the results of jealous boyfriends, and it won't end well for anyone. And besides, it'll only be a couple more years before we can be together forever."
I sit up in surprise. "Wait, really?"
"Yes. I just found out myself. It'll be rather messy, I'm afraid. But some things just can't be helped." My lover shrugged. "But don't jump the gun, alright? It could mess things up if we're not careful."

It takes everything inside me not to blurt out twenty different responses at once. But as I'm trying to figure out what to say first. I hear the door bursts open, almost completely coming off its hinges by the amount of force applied.

"Huh, looks like the paramedics are here." I sigh again as the paramedics quickly start attempting to resuscitate my body. I sigh, as I start feeling the tug back into the living world, our time together coming to a close. Death embraces me one last time. "I was hoping they'd take their time." I say, putting my arms around him.

"I know. I did as well." Death tells me. The pull is becoming stronger now. "But never forget that I love you."
"I love you too." is the last thing I can say before I'm pulled back into the living world.

到自己被他的眼神融化了。

「相信我，我明白你的感受，但我不會太嫉妒她。我看過不少吃醋的男朋友，對任何人來說都不會是好的結局。啊，對了，我們還有幾年就可以永遠在一起了。」

我驚訝地坐起來：「甚麼？真的嗎？」

「嗯，我剛剛發現的。不過恐怕那樣會比較麻煩，但有些事情是一定要做的。」我的情人聳聳肩：「但不要操之過急，知道嗎？如果我們大意的話，事情就會很麻煩了。」

我竭盡全力，按捺著內心二十個不同的反應，不讓它們爆發出來。但是，正當我在想首先應該說些甚麼時，我聽到門突然被撞開，大力得幾乎把門撞至脫落。

「嗄，醫護人員好像已經到了。」我又嘆了口氣，因為護理人員很快就會開始嘗試復甦我的身體。當我開始感覺到要被拉回凡間，我們相處的時間就要結束了，我嘆了口氣。死神最後一次擁抱我。「我真希望他們會慢慢來。」我挽著他的手臂說。

「我知道，我也希望。」死神跟我說，但拉力愈來愈強了。「但永遠不要忘記我愛你。」

「我也愛你。」這是我被拉回凡間之前，我能說的最後一句話。

They Got the Definition Wrong

It has been said that the definition of insanity is "doing the same thing over and over and expecting different results". I understand the sentiment behind the saying, but it's wrong.

I entered the building on a bet. I was strapped for cash and didn't buy into the old legends of the hotel to begin with, so fifty bucks was more than enough to get me do it. It was simple. Just reach the top floor, the 45th floor, shine my flashlight from a window.

The hotel was old and broken, including the elevator, so that meant hiking up the stairs. So up the stairs I went. As I reached each platform, I noted the old brass plaques displaying the floor numbers. 15, 16, 17, 18. I felt a little tired as I crept higher, but so far, no ghosts, no cannibals, no demons. Piece of cake.

I can't tell you how happy I was as I entered that last stretch of numbers. I joyfully counted them aloud at each platform. 40,41,42,43, 44, 44. I stopped and looked back down the stairs. I must have miscounted, so I continued up. 44. One more flight. 44. And then down ten flights. 44. Fifteen flights. 44.

他們的定義錯了

據說，精神錯亂的定義是「重複做著同一件事而期待著不同的結果」。我明白這句話的意思，但是那是錯的。

我跟別人打賭，所以走進了酒店。我超級缺錢，而且又不相信那些甚麼老掉牙的酒店都市傳說，所以跟我賭五十美元簡直是太慷慨了。那任務很簡單，只要到達頂樓 45 樓，在窗戶打開手電筒使它發光就行了。

那酒店又破又舊，連電梯也壞了，那就是說我要爬樓梯了，於是我就去了走樓梯。當我到達每一層時，我看到老舊的銅板寫著樓層號碼。15，16，17，18。我走得愈來愈高，我有點累了，但到目前為止，沒有鬼、沒有食人族、沒有惡魔，我輕而易舉就爬上去了。

當我走到最後幾層的時候，那種高興簡直非筆墨所能形容。我每走一層都會興高采烈地大聲數著，40，41，42，43，44，44。我停下來，回頭看著樓梯。我一定是數錯了，所以我繼續向上走。再上一層。44。然後下十層。44。十五層。44。

And so it's been for as long as I can remember. So really, insanity isn't doing something repeatedly and expecting different results. It's knowing that the results will never ever change; that each door leads to the same staircase, to the same number. It's realizing you no longer fall asleep. It's not knowing whether you've been running for days or weeks or years. It's when the sobbing slowly turns into laughter.

然後我只記得自己一直重複著這個動作，所以真的，精神錯亂不是重複做著同一件事而期待著不同的結果，而是知道結果永遠不會改變——每個門都是通向相同的樓梯，顯示著相同的數字；那是當你意識到你不會再睡著的時候；那是當你不知道你到底跑了幾天、幾週還是幾年的時候；當啜泣聲漸漸變成笑聲的時候。

This Story Does Not Have a Twist

This story does not have a twist. You won't find out that I'm really the killer at the end. Because I'm telling you so from the beginning. I am the killer.

I was the one who killed him.

I was the one who scouted out the old man hobbling along while out walking with my son.

I was the one who wanted to follow him down the street that day.

I was the one who had brought a pair of scissors along to do the killing.

I was the one who followed him into the alleyway, leading my six year old boy in hand.

I was the one who stabbed him thirty–six times.

I was the one who consoled my crying child.

I was the one who made him promise to lie to protect me.

Just please believe me. This story does not have a twist. I am the killer.

Author: Noah Mester

這個故事沒有大逆轉劇情

這個故事沒有大逆轉劇情。你不需要看到最後才發現我真的是兇手。因為我從一開始就告訴你，我就是兇手。

我就是殺死他的人。

我就是那個和我兒子一起走著的時候，看上了那個一瘸一拐的老頭子的人。

我就是那天企圖在街上跟蹤他的那個人。

我就是那個帶著一把剪刀走去殺人的人。

我就是那個牽著我那六歲的兒子，跟蹤他進入小巷的人。

我就是那個刺了他三十六次的人。

我就是那個安慰我那正在哭的孩子的人。

我就是那個讓他答應會說謊來保護我的人。

請相信我，這個故事沒有大逆轉劇情。我就是兇手。

True Love

There's this girl I like...

She's pretty. Really pretty. Smart too. I can talk to her for hours – and I do! I'm lucky I guess. We've been friends since we were kids. But I don't think she feels the same about me.

I mean... I kinda got the hint when she started telling me about boys she did like. But I hoped it'd be like those sappy romantic comedies. Where the girl thinks she found Mr. Right, but dumps him last minute for her best friend. Which is me. I am her best friend.

But that didn't happen. They got married anyways. So I had to step up and be a man. I had to show her that she was wrong. That we were right.

Being her best friend, it was too easy to lead her away to her new home. Too easy to avoid suspicion. Her bastard of a husband is even taking the fall!

Someday she'll understand. Someday, we'll be a happier family. Someday we'll have kids too. And I can only hope they would get along just as well as my sister and I did growing up.

真愛

我有個很喜歡的女孩。

她很漂亮，真的很漂亮，又很聰明。我可以跟她聊上幾個小時，而我真的有跟她聊過這麼久！我們從小就是很好的朋友，但我不認為她也像我喜歡她一樣喜歡我。

我意思是……在她跟我説她喜歡哪種男生時，我好像聽懂了她的暗示。但我希望她會像那些愚蠢的浪漫喜劇女主角般，以為自己找到如意郎君，到了最後關頭，還是會為了她最好的朋友而跟那個男生分手。我希望她會為了我跟他分手，因為我是她最好的朋友。

但那只是我的幻想，他們最後還是結婚了。所以我要將行動升級，我要做個男子漢。我要讓她知道她選錯了，而跟我在一起才是對的。

作為她最好的朋友，帶她離開她的新家實在是輕而易舉。也沒有人會懷疑我。她那混蛋老公輸給我了！

終有一天她會明白的。終有一天，我們會是更開心的一家人。終有一天，我們也會有孩子。我希望我的子女會像我和妹妹般，相親相愛地成長。

Watch Out for Pet Thieves

There's been an epidemic of pet thieves in my town, as of late.

They operate at night, breaking into people's backyards and accosting distracted pet owners on the street. No one knows for sure why they want our pets so badly. But, whatever reason it is, they're not getting their hands on mine.

My night started out like any other. After eating dinner and watching some TV, I grabbed Bailey's leash to take him for a walk. The scamp raced into the room and sat bolt upright, panting excitedly. Bailey loves walks. Living in a secluded town in rural Utah, I'd always felt safe walking around after dark. Neighbours waved hello or stopped to pet Bailey, but otherwise went peacefully about their business. Trouble only ever occurred when out–of–towners showed up. They were the ones stealing our pets – I was sure of it.

The night continued. I ran into my neighbour, Samantha, and we stopped to discuss the recent thefts while Bailey and Fifi sniffed around. Samantha agreed that it was probably transients behind the abductions, although she didn't seem too worried by them. Bailey and I were only a block away from home when I finally spotted one: the silhouette of a pet thief, crouched behind a veil of bushes.

提防寵物盜賊

近來我的城鎮流行著一股寵物盜竊潮。

那些小偷會在晚上行動，闖進人們的後園，又在大街上跟寵物的主人搭訕，使他們分心。沒有人確實知道他們那麼想要我們寵物的原因。但無論他們有甚麼原因，我也不會讓他們偷走我的寵物。

今晚跟平常一樣。我一如以往地吃完晚飯，看過電視，就拿起頸帶帶 Bailey 外出。那頑皮的傢伙馬上衝過來，坐直身子，興奮得氣喘吁吁的。Bailey 超愛出外的！雖然住在這個與世隔絕的小鎮，但就算入黑後我也感到很安心。鄰居們也一如以往地跟 Bailey 揮手問好，或是停下來摸摸牠，再不然就是靜靜地做著自己的事。外來客出現時就是最麻煩的時候，我敢肯定，他們就是那些要偷走我們寵物的人。

我和 Bailey 繼續走著，碰到了鄰居 Samantha。我們停了下來討論最近小偷的事，Bailey 和 Fifi 就在附近嗅來嗅去。Samantha 也認同那可能是綁架行動的其中一環，然而她看起來不太擔憂。Bailey 跟我走了不遠，只離我們家一個街區之遙，我發現了一個像寵物小偷的身影蹲在灌木叢後面。

Out of the corner of my eye, I could see him clicking away intently. He was taking photos of Bailey.

That was it. Enough was enough.

I tied Bailey to a lamppost, snuck around the corner, and watched. The thief was cautious, as if he expected a trap, but soon threw caution to the wind and darted forwards anyway. Seemingly recognising the man, Bailey whined incessantly. Strangely, the thief echoed this emotion, tears streaming down his face as he grappled with Bailey's leash. Before he could make any more headway, I stepped out and revealed myself. The thief threw his head up at me, startled. His fearful expression quickly turned to rage.

"What the fuck have you sick people done to my brother?!" he screamed, attempting to shield the whimpering, naked man tied to the pole. I stared back at him, blankly. Typical outsider.

The local sheriff caught up to the thief soon enough. Thankfully for the town, his petnapping days are over. We'll find use for him yet, just like Bailey and the others.

Pet thieves always make the best pets.

我眼角瞥到他在專心地按著按鈕……他正在拍攝 Bailey 的照片……

夠了，我受夠了！

我把 Bailey 綁在一根燈柱旁，然後自己拐到角落裡觀察著。那個小偷謹慎得彷似預計到會有陷阱般，但他的謹慎很快就隨風而去，不顧一切急步衝向 Bailey。看來 Bailey 認得那個男人，不停地低叫著。奇怪的是，那小偷也有同樣的情緒，一邊抓住 Bailey 的頸帶，眼淚一邊從他臉頰流下來。不等他再有甚麼行動之前，我走了出來站在他面前。那小偷抬起頭看著我，驚訝不已。但他驚慌的表情很快就變成了憤怒。

「你們他媽的對我弟弟做甚麼了？！」他咆哮著，嘗試保護那個被綁在柱子上、啜泣著的裸體男子。我冷冷地瞪回他。典型的外來客。

城內的警長很快把他抓起來了。多得這個小鎮的幫忙，他偷竊寵物的生涯就此結束。我們會找到他的用途，就像 Bailey 和其他人一樣。

寵物小偷永遠都能成為最棒的寵物。

Frantic Awakening
心寒覺悟

Annoying Neighbour

I used to live in a small building downtown. One of the reasons I moved out was the bad neighborhood, including this guy in the apartment right over mine. It was a weird looking fella who mostly kept to himself. Around midnight though, there was frequently a strange noise that got on my nerves. It wasn't loud, to be fair, but I have really light sleep so it was hard to get my eyes shut with those little bumping sounds going on and on. It reminded me of high heels walking about, but not as loud, as if the person causing the noise was actually trying to be silent. After a few days, I realized the pattern was always the same, like a recording played over and over with random intervals in between. And that went on for the best part of a year, always the same sequence of bumps, slowly tattooed into my mind, sometimes for hours straight during the night.

It was only several years later, helping my daughter with her homework, that I learned a little bit of morse code. She knocked on the table with her knuckles and a shiver immediately went through my spine as I recognized that exact pattern.

When I asked her what it meant, she laughed. "It's the easiest one, daddy" she said. "It's the one to call for help."

Author: Gabriel Oro

惱人的鄰居

我以前住在市中心的一間小房子，但後來搬走了，其中一個原因是因為鄰居都很惱人，尤其是住我樓上的那個傢伙，他是個很少出門、樣子也不討好的傢伙。每當夜深人靜的時候，總是有些奇怪的聲音吵著我，令我精神繃緊。説句公道話，其實它不是很大聲，只是我睡得很淺，有半點兒聲音我都睡不著，更何況是那些不斷重複、碰撞的聲音。那些聲音令我想起高跟鞋走路的聲音，但又沒有那麼大聲，就像是製造聲音的人不想被發現似的，把聲音壓得很小聲。幾天之後，我發現那個聲音總是重複著同一個節奏，就像錄音帶不斷重播著，間中又停頓一會。最「精彩」的是，經過每晚的折騰，有時夜裡連續幾個小時的吵著，這個聲音就漸漸烙在我腦海中。

幾年之後，因為要教女兒做功課，我學會了一點摩斯密碼。她用指關節敲打著桌子，我背脊馬上颼來一陣寒意。我認得這個節奏……

我問她那代表甚麼意思，她笑著回答：「爸爸，這個是最簡單的喔，是用來求救的。」

Google Now

I am not very good with technology, so when Google Now updates things without my knowledge, it scares me a bit.

At first it was only routes and nearby eateries.

Last month, while leaving work, it showed me a different route home. Assuming heavy traffic on the usual route, I took it. It took me about an hour. When I got home, the news channel was flashing with an accident on my usual route… from five minutes ago.

The other day I was out shopping, when Google Now alerted me of a florist nearby which sold bouquets especially for funerals. I brushed it off as a promotional offer. That very day, I received news that one of my friends had died from sudden kidney failure. At her funeral, I saw many floral bouquets from the florist from Google Now.

Now, as I'm sitting on the bathroom floor, run out of my depression medicines, and wondering why Google Now didn't remind me to buy more, I watch as it updates itself again.

Google Search results for **Quick, painless ways to kill yourself.**

Author: Raka Mukherjee

Google 即時資訊

我不善於操作科技產品，所以當 Google 即時資訊在我不知情的情況下更新內容時，實在嚇怕了我。

起初它只會提供一些路線和附近餐館的資料。

上個月我準備下班回家，Google 顯示了一條不同的路線給我參考。考慮到平常回家的路線很繁忙，於是就走了它提供的路線，花了差不多一小時就回到家。當我回到家時，新聞正在報導我平常回家的路上發生了意外，而且只是五分鐘前。

又有一天，我出去買東西，Google 即時資訊提示我附近有間花店有賣葬禮用的花。我看有促銷優惠就買下來了。同一天的稍後時間，我就收到消息說有位朋友因為腎衰竭過世了。在她的葬禮上，我看到許多花束都是來自 Google 即時資訊提供的那家花店。

現在，我坐在浴室的地板上，抑鬱藥都給我吃光了。我在想為甚麼 Google 沒有提醒我買藥，然後我看著它再次自動更新了。

Google 搜索結果顯示——**快速、無痛的自殺方法**。

Timekeeper

He had been given the watch on his tenth birthday. It was an ordinary grey plastic wristwatch in every respect except for the fact that it was counting down. "That is all of the time you have left in the world, son. Use it wisely." And indeed he did. As the watch ticked away, the boy, now a man, lived life to the fullest. He climbed mountains and swam oceans. He talked and laughed and lived and loved. The man was never afraid, for he knew exactly how much time he had left.

Eventually, the watch began its final countdown. The old man stood looking over everything he had done, everything he had built. 5. He shook hands with his old business partner, the man who had long been his friend and confidant. 4. His dog came and licked his hand, earning a pat on the head for its companionship. 3. He hugged his son, knowing that he had been a good father. 2. He kissed his wife on the forehead one last time. 1. The old man smiled and closed his eyes.

Then, nothing happened. The watch beeped once and turned off. The man stood standing there, very much alive. You would think that in that moment he would have been overjoyed. Instead, for the first time in his life, the man was scared.

Author: Joseph Dean

計時器

他在十歲生日時得到這隻錶。那是隻灰色塑膠腕錶，各方面都很普通，不過它是倒著計時的。「那就是你在人世所剩的時間，好好善用吧。」而他真的有好好善用時間。隨著手錶滴答滴答的倒數著，那男孩現已成了男人，充實地過著他的人生。他攀過無數的山、游過無數的海；他說過、笑過、活過、愛過。這個男人無所畏懼，因為他清楚知道自己還剩多少時間。

終於，手錶開始最後的倒數了，已變成老伯伯的他回顧著一生以來做過的一切、建立過的一切。五。他跟生意上的老伙伴、長久以來的好朋友、好知己握了手。四。他的狗走過來舔舔他的手，他很感激狗狗一直以來的陪伴，於是摸摸牠的頭。三。他抱抱兒子，深知自己當了個好爸爸。二。他在妻子的額頭上留下了最後一吻。一。老伯伯笑著合上眼睛。

然後，甚麼也沒有發生。手錶「嗶」了一聲就關掉了。老伯伯仍然好端端的站在那裡。你可能會想那時候他應該會喜出望外。然而，這卻是他人生中第一次感到害怕。

Wait, Something's Not Right

A sound wakes you up, sounded like a knock on your front door. It's way past midnight, you're lying on the sofa with the TV on static. The house is dark, the lights are off. You're all alone. You look out the window, see there's a full moon, shining its light through the glass pane.

You get up and head towards the front door. You look through the peephole. No one outside. You open the door. Find no one. You check around the porch. Still no one. Maybe kids were playing tricks on you.

Annoyed, you shut the door, turn off the TV, close the window, and head upstairs to your bedroom for the night.

等等，有點不妥

有些聲音喚醒了你，聽起來像是前門傳來的敲門聲。過了午夜已經很久了，你躺在沙發，電視靜止著。房子很暗，燈都關掉了，只有你自己一人。你望向窗外，看著那滿月的光線穿透了玻璃窗。

你站起來，向前門走去。你從窺視孔裡望向門外，沒有人在外面。你打開門，找不到任何人。你走到門廊到處查看，還是沒有人。也許是孩子們在惡作劇吧。

懊惱的你關上門，關掉電視機，關上窗戶，然後走到樓上，回到睡房度過餘下的晚上。

Artificial Intelligence is a Real Threat

Or so we thought.

That's why we made hoops and jumps to make sure they'd never get smarter than us. That's why we invented the Turing Test. It was the ultimate failsafe: If an AI passed the turing test, we'd instantly shut it down. Shut everything down, rip the batteries out, leave it no power source. No way we were letting a Terminator situation happen, even remotely.

So, when everyday machines actually gained control and shut the servers down, locked us out, took control and started the human extinction, we had a lot of time to figure out how we missed it, how could this have happened.

It wasn't until more than half of humanity was wiped out before we realized where we went wrong.

A computer smart enough to pass the Turing test will also be smart enough to fail it.

人工智能是個真實危機

或者我們是這麼認為。

因此我們制定了很多規範，以確保它們永遠不會比我們更聰明。這也是為甚麼我們發明了用來測試機器有沒有具備人類智能的「圖靈測試」。也就是最後把關的保障機制：如果某個 AI 通過了圖靈測試，我們會立即關閉它。我們會關掉它所有裝置，拆掉電池，不讓它接通任何電源。我們不容許有像《未來戰士》般的情況發生，即使情況極輕微也不允許。

所以，當我們日常用的機器真的得到了控制權，它們關掉伺服器、把我們鎖起來，控制並開始剷除人類的時候，我們還有很多時間來弄清楚我們是沒有發現錯處，以致怎麼會發生此等事情。

當一半以上的人類被清除的時候，我們才意識到哪裡出錯了。

電腦既然聰明得可以通過圖靈測試，它也可以聰明得不通過測試。

First Day of School

Rosie fidgeted with the zipper on her flowery backpack as she waited for the bus to arrive and take her to school. Behind her, mom and dad were just as nervous but willed themselves not to show it. They wanted Rosie's first day to be an exciting new experience, not filled with anxiety.

They could've just taken her themselves as they didn't live far from school, but they wanted their sweet daughter to make friends and meet new people. The bright, yellow bus stopped in front of their house before they could change their minds, though.

The bus was surprisingly empty and that only added to the family's nerves.

After a big group hug and multiple kisses from mom and dad, Rosie entered the bus, picking a seat toward the front.

The plump driver waved at mom and dad, hardly making eye contact. The door squeaked shut behind their treasured, baby girl. Mom wiped away a small tear as she and her husband watched the bus disappear around the corner far down the street.

"She's going to have a great day" dad comforted mom with a forehead kiss.

開學日

Rosie 等著校巴來接她上學，沒趣的她玩弄著她那個花花背包上的拉鏈。在她身後的是她的爸爸媽媽，他們雖然強裝輕鬆，但始終難掩緊張的神情。他們希望今天開學日會是 Rosie 一個精彩的新里程，不想她帶著緊張的心情上學。

Rosie 一家住的地方離學校不遠，她父母其實可以親自送她回校，但因為想寶貝女兒可以認識新朋友，所以只好陪她等校巴。等不及 Rosie 爸爸媽媽改變主意，亮麗的黃色校巴已駛至他們家門前。

可是，那校巴竟然空無一人，這使 Rosie 爸媽更加緊張。Rosie 和爸爸媽媽擁抱和親吻過後，就上了校巴，選了個前排的位置坐下。

那圓滾滾的司機向 Rosie 爸媽揮手，但幾乎沒有眼神接觸。車門嘎吱一聲關上了，無情地把他們和珍而重之的寶貝女兒隔開了。Rosie 爸媽看著校巴駛遠，最後消失在街角之中，媽媽輕輕擦走眼角的淚水。

「她今天一定會過得很好的。」爸爸輕吻了媽媽額頭安慰著她。

"I know" mom agreed, not sounding as confident. "I'm going to shower" she finished, heading inside.

As dad's footsteps entered their home, a loud honk startled him. His stomach emptied into his throat as he turned around to see a different bus, loaded with happy students, idling at the foot of his driveway.

The big door slid open.

"Good morning, Mr. Thomas" the elderly bus driver asked with a pleasant smile like that of a loving grandmother. "Is Rosie ready for her first day?"

「我知道。」媽媽雖不太安心，但還是接受了現實：「我去洗個澡。」説罷就向家中走去。

正當爸爸準備踏入家門，一下響亮的汽車喇叭聲把他嚇了一跳。

他轉頭去看，卻被眼前的畫面嚇得幾乎吐出來了：他看見一輛完全不同、滿載著快樂學童的校巴，停靠在他的車道上。

車門打開了。

「早安，Thomas 先生！」年老的校巴司機面露笑容，如慈祥的老婆婆般問道：「Rosie 準備好第一天上學了嗎？」

Dispatch

The radio crackled to life.

"Hello? Rob, are you there?" asked a voice from the radio.
"Bill, is that you?" I replied surprised.
"Course it's me. Don't you remember your childhood friend's voice?"
"Yeah, of course. It's just been a while. How's life been treating you, huh? How's the wife and kids?"
"The wife and kids are fine. And life hasn't been treating me half as well as it's treated you, Mr. Big–shot astronaut."
"Yeah," I said sitting back in my chair and sighing, " I guess it has."

We shoot the shit for what seems like minutes, but when I check the clock it's actually been a couple of hours. They must have checked the clocks on their end too because Bill's voice suddenly get's serious.

"Rob, they've been telling me weird things about you."
"Yeah, like what?"
"That you've gone mad. That you've killed everyone on the station."
"That's just not true Bill."
"Yes it is," he shot back.

電訊通報

無線電劈哩啪啦地響了起來。

「喂？ Rob，你在嗎？」無線電的聲音問道。
「Bill ？是你嗎？」我回答道。
「當然是我，你不記得你的童年朋友的聲音嗎？」
「嗯，當然記得咯。也不是很久沒聯絡。最近生活怎樣啦？妻子和孩子挺好嗎？」
「老婆和孩子都很好，但生活就沒有你一半好啦，大人物太空人先生。」
「嗯，」我坐在椅子上，嘆了一口氣：「是這樣吧。」

我們一直吹著牛皮，好像只是十幾分鐘的事，但是當我看鐘時，原來已經過了幾個小時。他們也應該看了鐘，因為 Bill 的聲音突然變得嚴肅。

「Rob，他們一直在告訴我有關你的奇怪事情。」
「是嗎，例如呢？」
「你發瘋了，殺死了太空站裡的所有人。」
「你不是真的 Bill。」
「我是。」他很快回答。

I take a look at the chair next to me where the body of what used to be Astronaut Shepard is decomposing,

"Yes it is," I replied.
"Rob, these guys say they can get you help, you won't be punished or anything. You just have to come down, alright? You just have to come back to earth."
"You know Bill? Things get confused up here. Looking down on everyone makes it feel like you're a God. Like you can do anything you want," I pause for dramatic effect, "Every man has got a breaking point and I think I've reached mine. Tell my wife I love her. Goodbye."
"Wait, Rob…"

I turn off the radio. I suppose they'll get my 'wife' on next. A shame really, I was really enjoying talking to Bill. He was one of my closest friends growing up and I cried like a bitch at his funeral. Pretty sloppy on their part to not know Bill didn't have a wife or leave any kids, but I guess that's to be expected.

When that weird moon rock split open and those things crawled out and took over everyone's body, all they could do was scream and try to rip my guts out with their hands. The ones on earth must be smarter, they know if they send a shuttle up to get me then I'll destroy it with the station. What hurts one of them, hurts them all and so they've taken up

我看看我旁邊的椅子，那副曾經屬於太空人 Shepard 的身體正在腐化著。

「是的。」我回答。

「Rob，這些傢伙說他們可以幫你，你不會受到懲罰或發生任何事情。你只需要下來就可以了，好嗎？你只需要回到地球就好了。」

「Bill，你知道嗎？這裡所有東西都很混亂。往下看著大家，感覺就像上帝一樣。你可以做任何你想做的事，」我停了一下，營造戲劇效果：「每個人都有極限，我想我已經到達了我的極限。告訴我的妻子我愛她，再見。」

「Rob，等等……」

我關掉了無線電。我想他們下一次就會找來我「老婆」。真的很可惜，我真的很喜歡和 Bill 聊天。他是我其中一個最親密的朋友，我在他的葬禮上哭得像個孩子。他們也挺馬虎的，竟然不知道 Bill 沒有妻子或留下任何孩子，但我想正常人也會這樣猜測吧。

當那個奇怪的月亮岩裂開了，然後那些東西爬出來，控制了每個人的身體，他們所能做的只是尖叫，試圖用手把我的內臟扯出來。在地球的那些一定更聰明，他們知道如果派穿梭機來抓我，我就會將它連同太空站一起摧毀掉。只要傷害他

trying to convince me to come down willingly. I don't mind it though, things can get pretty lonesome up here, so it's nice to have someone to talk to. I think the isolation is getting to me though, sometimes I swear I hear screaming coming from the walls even though I know I'm the only one left. Sometimes I scream back.

So now, I guess it's a waiting game to see which runs out first:

The oxygen, my sanity or their patience.

們其中一個，其他都會受到牽連，所以他們寧願嘗試説服我自願下來。但我不介意，在這裡所有東西會變得很寂寞，所以有人跟我聊聊天也不錯。我感覺到孤獨感開始侵蝕我了，我發誓即使我知道自己是剩餘的唯一一個，但有時真的會聽到叫喊聲從牆壁傳來，而我也會回喊著。

所以現在，我想這是一場等待遊戲，看看哪樣會最先耗光：

氧氣、我的理智，還是他們的耐性。

My Dad was a Mortician

I remember a friend of mine tell me that thunder was clouds bumping together, he was proud when he told me that; he was also twenty–six. It's amazing what we believe when told at such a young age.

When I was thirteen, my dad said I was old enough to help him out. My dad was a mortician. I remembered the sleepless nights in the week leading up to it. The nightmares were horrific, and they never stopped. Before I didn't know exactly what he did, but I knew it involved dead bodies. I cried, but he said I was a man now, and this was something a man does, I believed him.

I worked that job for three years until I was sixteen and left home. To say it scarred me would be an understatement, but I did my best to get on with life. And I am proud to say I did okay, no lasting side effects to all that death.

I hadn't seen my dad since, until today, and now I am forty. I looked down at his body.

"Yeah, that's him," I said to the man in the lab coat.

He thanked me and pulled the sheet over my father's face.

我爸是個殯葬業者

我想起有個朋友告訴我雷鳴是因為雲朵撞在一塊，他講的時候還很驕傲呢！當時他也是二十六歲，那個年紀我們聽說甚麼都會深信不疑，真有趣呢。

我十三歲的時候，我爸說我年紀夠大，可以幫他的忙了。我爸是個殯葬業者。我猶記得因為幫爸爸的忙，弄得我那些晚上都睡得不好，那些惡夢非常可怕，而且不會停止。我以前還不懂爸爸的職業是甚麼一回事，我只知道是跟死人有關。我哭了，但爸爸說我已經是個男子漢了，而這些就是男子漢要做的事，我相信了他。

直到我十六歲搬出來自己住之前，我一直在做那個工作，做了三年。如果說那個工作對我來說是個陰影，那肯定只是輕描淡寫。但我可以很自豪地說我沒甚麼事，面對過那些死亡的氣息之後也沒有副作用。

但之後我就沒有再見過爸爸了，直到今天才看見他，我現在已經四十歲了。我低頭看著他的身體。

「對，就是他。」我向穿著實驗袍的男人說。

他跟我道謝過後就把被單蓋過爸爸的臉。

“That’s my dad alright. He was a mortician too, you know?”

The man ignored me and filled out his paperwork.

“This place is so quiet? How do you keep it so silent?”

He looked up from his clipboard and smiled, “Well the residents here don’t talk much.”
“But what about all the ones still alive, where do you keep them?”

He gave me a strange look.

“Well if they are living, they hardly belong here do they...” he said trailing off.

That’s when it hit me, I don’t think my dad was a mortician after all.

「他是我爸，他以前也是個殯葬業者啊，你知道嗎？」

那男人無視我的説話，只是默默地填寫文件。

「這裡好安靜啊……你是怎麼保持這裡的寧靜啊？」

他不再看著筆記板，抬頭看著我，笑著回答：「喔，這裡的『居民』都不太多話。」
「但是，那些還活著的，你把他們安置到哪裡去？」

他一臉詫異的看著我。

「唔……如果他們尚在人世，就不會在這裡出現了，對嗎？」他邊説邊離開。

就是他這句話，令我不再認為我爸是個殯葬業者了。

My Roommate Works Night Shifts

My roommate works night shifts. I rarely see him, because when I get up to go to work, he's still at work. When he gets up to go to work, I'm asleep. When I get home from work, he's asleep. When he gets home from work, I'm still at work. Outside of weekends, we only communicate via text.

We don't socialise much, so he came up with an idea for something we could do. We put a chess set on the coffee table. He made the first move, and the plan was that when I got up in the morning, I would see his move and then make mine. When he got up in the evening, he'd see my move and then make his, and so on. Even though we didn't see each other during the game, it was quite fun.

After about a month, he made a few very good moves and gained the upper hand. One morning I woke up to find that he'd checkmated me. I pulled out my phone to text him congratulations, and I saw he'd sent a text to me.

"Hey man! Sorry I didn't let you know beforehand, but I've been out of town for the past week. If you were wondering why I haven't made a move, that's why."

Author: William Roland–Batty

我那上夜班的室友

我的室友是值夜班的。我們幾乎都見不到面，因為當我起床去上班的時候，他還未下班；換他起床去上班的時候，我就在睡覺；到我下班的時候，就換他在睡覺了；到他下班了，我還在上班。除了週末以外，我們只會傳訊息來溝通。

我們很少交流，所以他提議可以找點甚麼一起做。於是我們在茶几上放了一個棋盤。他走了第一步棋，在我隔天早上起床時，我就會看到他的棋步，然後我就走我的棋步；換他晚上起床時，就會看到我的棋步，然後走他的棋步，如此類推。即使我們在棋賽中沒有看到對方的樣子，那也是個很有趣的經歷。

大約一個月後，他走了幾步高明的棋步，而且佔著上風。有一天早上醒來的時候，我發現他已經將軍了。我拿出手機打算給他道賀，然後我看到他給我發了一個短訊。

「嘿，對不起，我沒有事先知會你，但我已經在上個星期離開鎮子了，如果你在想為甚麼我沒有走下一步的話，這就是原因了。」

My Sincerest Thanks

Dear Sir,

It has recently come to my attention that I have been negligent in areas of etiquette. Particularly in the composition and dissemination of letters of thanks. Therefore, without further delay, allow me to express my gratitude.

Thank you for the package containing the toy clown's head and parking meter faceplate. I found the clown head to be unique, with its interesting paint job and crown of animal fur. The faceplate is certainly something that I was lacking. I found it all the more interesting given that it evidently came from the street in front of my apartment.

Thank you for the package containing seventeen live roaches. Though I'll admit to something of a shock upon opening the box, my cat did enjoy the subsequent hunt.

Thank you for the envelope containing photographs of myself in various state of undress. It called to my attention the poor state of my bedroom curtains, and ultimately allowed me to splurge on a new set.

Thank you for the package containing my cat's paws and tail. It was certainly unexpected, but I am grateful to you for demonstrating the frailty of life.

最衷心的道謝

敬啟者：

我注意到我最近在禮節方面有點疏忽了，特別是在撰寫和發布感謝信方面。所以，我不想再延遲，請允許我表示我的感謝之情。

感謝您那裝著玩具小丑頭和停車咪錶面板的包裹。我發現那個小丑頭是獨一無二的，有著有趣的油漆繪畫和用動物毛製成的頂部。那面板正正就是我缺乏的東西，我發現更有趣的地方是，它顯然是從我公寓前面的街道拿下來的。

感謝您那裝著十七隻活蟑螂的包裹。我承認雖然打開盒子的時候有點嚇倒了，但之後我的貓咪確實很喜歡追捕牠們。

感謝您那封裝滿了我在不同狀態下被拍到的裸體照片信。它提醒了我，我睡房的窗簾很糟糕，最終讓我花了一大筆錢換了一套新窗簾。

感謝您那裝著我貓咪爪子和尾巴的包裹。這當然是意想不到的，但我很感激你演示了生命的脆弱。

Thank you for the package containing the bloody police badge and lock of hair. It was quite unfair of me to involve the local authorities, when all you are doing is sending me gifts. I understand that now, and I appreciate the thought.

Finally, thank you for your letter today. Had you not sent it, I would not have seen my ungrateful behavior for what it was. Etiquette is important, and I would be remiss for not adhering to it.

Yours in sincerest gratitude,
Julie

感謝您那裝著血淋淋的警察徽章和一撮頭髮的包裹。這樣涉及地方當局的話不太公平了，因為你只是在送禮物給我而已。我現在明白了，而我也很欣賞這個想法。

最後，謝謝你今天的信。如果你沒有寄給我的話，我不會察覺到我的行為是忘恩負義的。禮儀很重要，如果我沒有遵守就是我的不當。

奉上我最衷心的感謝，

Julie 上

Rotary Phone

"She's awake," I said to the man next to me.
"Did she take her tablets?"
"Yes, at 20:01 last night, all five," I replied, checking the notes left for me.

We watch as the girl stretches. She pulls back the covers and stands.

"What are we looking for?" my colleague asks.
"Anything that would suggest she's violent towards others or herself," I press the intercom, "Sally, she's awake."

We wait now.

Sally knocks on the door. The girl opens it and invites her in. Sally offers her tray. The girl picks up the paper cup filled with pills and raises it to her mouth. She then takes the cup of water and downs it. I smile, I think she's ready. I make a note and we continue to watch.

Sally leaves the room. The girl begins to undress. We avert our eyes; when we look back, she's fully dressed.

Something alerts her attention. She picks up the phone in the corner of the room. I sigh, my colleague shakes his head.

轉盤式電話

「她醒了。」我跟旁邊的男人說。
「她吃藥了沒？」
「吃了，昨晚八點零一分吃了全部五顆。」我邊查看著那些留給我的筆記邊回答。

我們望著那個女孩伸了個懶腰，然後拉開被子站起來。

「我們要找甚麼？」同事問我。
「找證據證明她對別人或自己有暴力行為。」我按下對講機：「Sally，她醒了。」

我們等待著。

Sally 敲了敲門，女孩開門讓她進去。Sally 把托盤拿給女孩，女孩拿起那個裝滿藥丸的紙杯，把藥丸倒進嘴裡。然後她拿起一杯水，把水喝掉。我微笑，我想她已經準備好了。我記錄下來，然後繼續觀察。

Sally 離開了房間。女孩開始脫衣服，我們迴避了一下。當我們再看她的時候，她已經換好衣服了。

有些東西引起了她的注意。她拿起放在房間角落的電話。我嘆了口氣，我的同事則搖搖頭。

"This is not necessarily a bad thing."
"It's not a good thing."
"It's not violent, it's a crutch."
"The phone isn't plugged in," he replies, making notes of his own.
"Turn up the volume," I ask.

The equipment hisses as the sensitivity increases.

"I'm fine mum, they are treating me very well. I don't know what I am going to do. I am looking forward to breakfast. Yes, biscuits and gravy today. No, I don't know if there will be sausages. I know they are my favourite. They are never as good as what you'd make for me. Okay, I'll speak to you later, I think Sally is coming back."

The girl puts the phone down and begins kicking her legs. I think about my son, about how much I miss him. She is going to be leaving us today, I am more than happy to approve her release. She will be going to her aunt's, but the medication seems to be doing the job well.

"She's still using the phone," my colleague says resigned.
"That's not a bad thing, remember what she was like? If that's how she's coping, how is it different from a security blanket or cigarettes?" I reasoned with him.

「這不一定是壞事。」
「但也不是好事。」
「那不是暴力，那是寄託。」
「那電話沒有接線。」他邊說邊寫筆記。
「調高音量。」我說。

隨著靈敏度的增加，播放設備嘶嘶作響。

「媽媽，我很好，他們對我很好。我不知道我該做甚麼。我在等吃早餐。對啊，今天吃餅乾配肉湯。不是不是，我不知道有沒有香腸。雖然這些都是我最愛吃的，但總不及你煮的好吃。好吧，Sally 回來了，我待會兒再跟你聊。」

女孩把手機放下，開始踢著腿。我想起我的兒子，想起我有多麼的掛念他。她今天就要離開我們了，我興高采烈地批准她獲釋。她會跟她姨姨生活，藥物也似乎有效了。

「她還是在用那個電話。」我的同事絕望地說著。
「那不是壞事，記得她之前是怎樣嗎？如果這是她的處理方式，那麼她和安全毯或香煙有甚麼不同？」我說服他。

"This will be on you," he said, shaking his head.
"Don't worry, I am still your doctor, I'll see you next week for our appointment," I said.

She smiled and left the building, entering her aunt's car, before disappearing off the property.

Her room looked larger as the movers took her furniture out. I always felt happy when a patient left in happy circumstances. I was about to close the door when I heard the sound that stopped me in my tracks.

I stared at the phone, not wanting to pick it up. Slowly, I reached for the handset.

"Hello?"
"Daddy? Is that you?"

I picked up the phone, confirmed it wasn't connected, and I panicked.

「那就看你了。」他搖搖頭說。
「不用擔心，我還是你的醫生，我們下星期再見。」我說。

她微笑著離開了大樓，進了姨姨的車，然後漸漸遠去。

搬運工把傢具移走了，使她的房間顯得更大。看著病人帶著愉快的心情離開，我也會感到高興。我正想關門離開的時候，聽見有些聲音，使我停下了腳步。

我盯著電話，不想接聽。我慢慢把聽筒拿到耳邊。

「喂？」
「爸爸？是你嗎？」

我拿起電話，確認它沒有接線後，我慌了……

She Never Lost the Ring

I married my wife, Amy, a decade ago. To mark our engagement, I gifted her a princess–cut sapphire ring with a silver band. Like her, the sapphire was one–of–a–kind and irreplaceable. Amy was beyond grateful, and promised that she would wear it forever. She even joked that the ring was wedged onto her finger so tightly that she couldn't take it off, even if she wanted to.

Despite this, several years into our marriage, Amy lost the ring.

Something about her changed after that. Almost overnight, Amy became wicked, vindictive and cruel. She would take any opportunity to undermine my self–confidence and make me feel as if I wasn't good enough for her. My once kind–hearted, soft–spoken wife now relished the chance to inflict pain. This behaviour carried over into how she treated our children. She became abusive towards them, screaming at them for the slightest of faults. Amy seemed to take a sick pleasure in this. It amazed me how someone could treat their own children, their own husband, so coldly.

This wasn't the same woman I fell in love with.

Eventually, I filed for divorce. I wasn't going to let my kids endure another second of this abuse, even if it was from a

她從來不會弄丟戒指

十年前我娶了 Amy 為妻。訂婚的時候，我送了一隻鑲有公主切割的方形藍寶石銀戒指給她。藍寶石跟她一樣，是獨一無二、不可替代的。Amy 非常感動，並答應我她會永遠戴著它。她甚至開玩笑説，這個戒指緊緊地楔住了她的手指，即使她想把它脱掉也不行。

儘管如此，我們結婚幾年之後，Amy 丟失了戒指。

在那天之後她變了。幾乎是一夜之間的事，Amy 變得邪惡、報復心強，而且很殘忍。她會用盡所有機會來打擊我的自信心，讓我覺得自己不夠好，配不起她。我那曾經善良、説話溫和的妻子，現在竟然很享受看著我受盡痛苦折磨。不只是對我，她對待孩子也是這樣兇惡。她變得對孩子們很粗暴，他們犯了半點錯誤就會被她大喊大叫地責罵。但 Amy 似乎從中找到了病態的愉快感。令我驚訝的是，竟然有人可以這般冷漠地對待自己的孩子和丈夫。

這不是我愛的那個女人。

最後，我提出離婚。即使那是我曾經愛過的女人，我也不會讓孩子忍受多一秒的虐待。令人驚訝的是，我提出單獨撫養孩子，Amy 並沒有反對。她只收拾了行裝，在訴訟過程還在進行中就已經消失了。

woman I once loved. Surprisingly, Amy didn't fight my appeal for sole custody. She packed her things and disappeared the moment proceedings were through.

While clearing out my belongings from our old house, I happened upon something that caught my interest. In the back of the shed, hidden behind several crates, was a steel drum that I had never noticed before. It was strange. There was no reason why Amy or myself would have needed a steel drum, especially not one this large. My curiosity getting the better of me, I approached it and pried the lid open.

I immediately recoiled as a wretched smell filled the shed. Inside the drum lay the skeletal, decaying remains of a woman. The corpse was long unrecognizable, and completely stripped of any clothing — with one exception on its left hand.

Still wrapped around a decomposing finger was a princess–cut sapphire ring with a silver band.

我在我們同住的舊房子裡收拾物品時，發現了一樣讓我感興趣的東西。在棚屋的後方，有個我從未注意過的鋼桶藏在幾個大貨箱後面。我覺得很奇怪，因為我和 Amy 都沒有理由需要一個鋼桶，特別是像這個那麼大的桶子。我的好奇心愈來愈旺盛，於是我向它走近，撬開了蓋子。

一種骯髒的氣味立即充滿了棚子。桶裡面放著一具的骸骨，是個腐爛的女性遺體。那具屍體已經無法識別，身上也沒有任何服飾——除了左手。

那腐爛的手指上仍然戴著鑲有公主切割的方形藍寶石銀戒指。

The Voices, They Never Leave You

I had them since I was a child, sometimes they seemed to come from the people around me, as if I could hear their thoughts; I'd shout at them, they'd look at me strangely and think I was mad.

I became so disruptive in school, my parents took me to the doctor who prescribed me so many different medications I can't remember. Some made me feel so sick, some like a zombie. In the end, when the medication didn't make me want to vomit or lose all my emotions, I pretended the voices were gone; I kept them to myself from then on.

It wasn't until my teenage years that I realised I could actually hear people's thoughts. Now that may sound like a gift, but it was a burden. I once stopped a girl committing suicide, however that just ended up with her in and out of psychiatric care. I'm not sure if she was better off now, or whether I should have let her do what she wanted in the first place.

Being out in public became an ordeal, so many different voices pushing past my own thoughts and taking center stage. It's impossible to think. Walking down the street hearing what people's first impressions are of me, *what an ugly fuck – ha, fat bastard – he looks depressed – if I looked like that I'd kill myself*

And my parents... Knowing what they really think of me. I

纏繞一生的聲音

我小時候就已經會聽到這些聲音，有時他們好像是我周圍的人，就像是我能聽見他們在想甚麼一樣。我會對著他們大叫，但他們會以奇怪的目光看著我，覺得我是神經病。

我在學校變得很頑皮，我的父母帶我去看醫生，他給我很多很多不同的藥物，多得我也記不清了。有些藥讓我覺得很不舒服，有些使我像喪屍一樣。最後，當那些藥物沒有再使我想嘔吐或失去所有的情緒時，我就假裝那些聲音已經消失了。從那時起，我沒有再跟任何人提起過這些聲音。

直到我十幾歲的時候，我才意識到原來自己真的可以聽見人們在想甚麼。雖然聽起來好像是超能力般奇妙，但其實是個負擔。我曾經阻止過一個想自殺的女孩，但是最後卻令她需要接受精神治療。我不知道她現在有沒有過得更好，還是我一早應該讓她自行了斷就好了。

到公共場所更成為了一種折磨，許多不同的聲音蓋過了我自己的想法，奪去了我的自主，使我沒辦法思考。走在街上，我聽見人們對我的第一印象：*好醜喔*、*哈，死胖子*、*他看起來很沮喪*、*如果我長成這樣我會寧願自殺*……

至於我的父母，我知道他們對我真正的看法，我不想再見他們了，尤其是聽過他們的看法之後。

couldn't see them again, not after what I heard.

When I graduated high school, I drove my car. Just drove. Into the desert. With my graduation present from my parents, I put down the first two month's rent on a house in the middle of nowhere. What bliss! No more voices. I took a part time job down at the hardware store.

Until a few weeks in, this man comes in looking shifty.

I like the look of that spade, looks damn sharp.

"Sharpest one we got," I said out loud, before putting my hands to my mouth.
Puzzled he asked, "You know about these?"
"Course I do, it's my job."
"I'll take it, and some of that duct tape."

I'm going to enjoy this I heard, as he took his equipment and left. I ignored it, it wasn't my business and I didn't care. I'd gone past caring.

That night I awoken by a muffled sound. I got up and went to the kitchen to get a drink, but I could still hear it.

el – elp – help

在我高中畢業後，我一直開著車，開到去沙漠。我以父母送給我的畢業禮物，在四下無人的地方租了個房子，付了頭兩個月的租金。太幸福了！沒有聲音了！然後我在五金店找了一份兼職工作。

直到幾個星期後，有個蛇頭鼠目的人走到店內。

我喜歡那個鏟子的造型，看起來很鋒利。

「那是我們這裡最鋒利的。」我大聲說了出來，然後掩著嘴巴。
他困惑地問：「你會這些嗎？」
「當然會啦，這是我的工作嘛。」
「我要這個，還有一些膠帶。」

我會很喜歡這個的，他拿著工具離開時我聽見這句話。我沒有理會它，這不關我事，我不在乎，我不會再關心其他人了。

那天晚上，我被一把低沉的聲音吵醒。我起來去廚房喝個飲料，但是我仍然聽到……

唔—命—救命……

My blood ran cold when I realised what it was. I thought back to the man, I could have stopped him.

I drove around looking for her, looking for some disturbed soil or something to indicate the ground had been touched.

I heard that woman's screams and pleas for seven days before it... changed.

That was just the first of many. I cannot escape the voices. I've been trying to talk back, to comfort them, or maybe I'm just trying to comfort myself.

當我意識到那是甚麼時，我頓時感到心驚膽寒。我想到了那個男人，我本來可以阻止他的。

我開著車，四處尋找她，看看地上有沒有一些被翻亂的泥土或地上有甚麼顯示到有人移動過的痕跡。

我聽著那個女人的尖叫聲和懇求聲聽了七天，然後它……改變了。

那只是許多人裡面的第一個，我避不開他們的聲音。我一直嘗試跟他們說話，安慰他們，或許我只是想安慰自己。

Internet Shopping

Please fill in or select an option from each of the following fields to place your order.

Sex: (Female)

Age Group:
☐ 18 – 19 ☐ 15 – 17 ☐ 10 – 14 ☑ <10
Eye Color: (Green)
Hair Color, Texture, Length: (Brown, straight, long)
Body Type:
☐ Emaciated ☐ Skinny ☑ Neutral ☐ Chubby ☐ Obese
Skin Tone:
☑ Pale ☐ Normal ☐ Tan ☐ Dark

Extras:
If female, pregnant? (No)
Physically Handicapped? (No)
Mentally Handicapped? (No)
Comatose? (No)
Amputee? (No)
Blind? (No)
Deaf? (No)
Mute? (Hell no.)
Deceased? If so, proper preservatives will be provided. (No)

網購

如欲下單，請填寫以下資料或從選項中打勾。

性別：（女）

年齡：☐ 18 - 19 歲　☐ 15 - 17 歲

　　　☐ 10 - 14 歲　☑ 10 歲或以下

眼睛顏色：（綠色）

頭髮顏色、髮質、長度：（楬色、直、長）

身形：

☐ 枯瘦　☐ 苗條　☑ 中等　☐ 豐滿　☐ 癡肥

膚色：

☑ 偏白　☐ 正常　☐ 偏深　☐ 很深

其他：

如是女性，是否懷孕？（不）

是否肢體殘障？（不）

是否智力缺陷？（不）

是否處於昏迷狀態？（不）

是否截肢者？（不）

是否視障？（不）

是否聽障？（不）

是否啞巴？（他媽的不。）

是否已死亡？如已死亡，本店將會提供適當的防腐劑。（不）

Would you like any accessories? If so, please specify:
(–collar)
(–whip)
(–knife)

What condition would you like your order to come in?
(Unconscious)

How would you like us to package your order?
(Boxed, bound, blindfolded, nude)

Would you like to place another order? With Premium, multiple orders can be sent to your location with guaranteed simultaneous arrival. (No)

Are you sure? (Yes)

Will you give us a rating on your satisfaction upon the arrival of your order? (Yes)

Subtotal: $1,456,782.45
Accessories Charge: $150.00
Tracking and Acquiring Fee: $1,389.77
Packaging Fee with Specifications: $875.50
Shipping Fee: $299.99
Total Cost: $1,459,497.71

需要加配飾品嗎？如有需要，請詳述：
（頸圈）
（鞭子）
（刀子）

您希望貨品運抵時是處於甚麼狀態？（神志不清）

您希望我們如何包裝您的貨品？
（盒裝，繩綁，蒙眼，裸體）

您想再下另一張訂單嗎？使用進階版可同時發送多個訂單，而且保證同時到達。（不）

您確定嗎？（是）

您會否在貨品運抵時替我們寫個滿意的評級？（會）

小計：$1,456,782.45
飾品費用：$150.00
跟踪及捕獲費用：$1,389.77
包裝連加工費用：$875.50
運費：$299.99
總計：$1,459,497.71

Thank you for placing an order. At the very soonest, your order will arrive in about one month. At the latest, six weeks.

You will not be permitted to physically track your order once it has been acquired and packaged, but you will receive consistent updates on its travel progress. If you have any questions or comments about your order, or if you have failed to receive your order, please, do not hesitate to notify us, and we will remedy any problems, as well as answer questions.

Have a nice day!

感謝您的訂單。您的訂單最快將於約一個月內，或最遲六個星期內到達。

如您的貨品已被獲取及打包，您將不能繼續跟蹤您的貨品，但您將會收到有關其運送進度的資料更新。如您對訂單有任何問題或意見，或者未能收到貨品，請隨時通知我們，我們樂意回答您的問題，並作出相應的補償。

祝您有愉快的一天！

Have Fun

We arrived in the ambulance and got out as quickly as we could.

"We need a neck brace and a stretcher," said Rick.
"I'm on it," Stuart replied.

I looked at the mangled body on the road, seeing it gasp for breath, knowing it was probably too late. But for that one time in a hundred, I crouched down next to them.

"Don't worry, we're here now. Where do you hurt?" I soothed.

The body just breathed; they appeared paralysed. The other paramedics returned with the stretcher and placed it next to the man, the victim of a hit and run.

Rick placed the neck–brace behind him and closed it shut.

"Help me lift him on, be careful, I think he may have broken his back or neck."

Stuart took one end and I the other. Over the loud speaker I heard the announcement.

"It's time for your mandatory pleasure period; have fun for the next 15 minutes."

玩得開心點

我們駕著救護車駛至，然後盡快從車廂跑出來。

「給我頸托和擔架。」Rick 說。
「收到。」Stuart 回答。

我望著那個躺在馬路上、被輾爛的軀體喘不過氣來，我就知道已經太遲了。我平常不會這樣做的，但今次我蹲在他旁邊。

「別擔心，現在有我們在。你哪裡受傷了嗎？」我安慰道。

那軀體呼吸著，但似乎幾近癱瘓了。其他救護人員帶著擔架回來，放在傷者旁邊，那個撞倒他的司機早就不見蹤影了。

Rick 幫他戴上頸托，然後把它牢牢的關緊。

「幫我抬他上去，小心點，他的背或頸子可能都斷了。」

我和 Stuart 一頭一尾地抬著擔架。然後擴音器傳來了廣播：「現在是強制遊樂時間，接下來的 15 分鐘，玩得開心點！」

我們同步丟下了擔架，開始嘻嘻哈哈地開起玩笑來。

We dropped the body in unison and began laughing and joking.

"Hey, guys, he's dying, please help me?" Rick pleaded.

We feigned a smile.

"What did you do last night, Stuart?" I asked.
"I had so much fun with the family," he responded smiling.
"Good, I had a lot of fun with my family too."
"Shit, I think we are losing him," Rick said panicked.
"Stop it!" I demanded, "Have fun!"
"Hahaha, I love it here. Do you know, I'm going to ride a horse after work?" I said laughing.
"Oh that does sound like fun, I'm going to," Stuart began before the sound of machine gun fire broke through our conversation.

The bullets landed in Rick in quick succession. His body lurched forward onto the man in the road.

"I think his dead body is suffocating the man," Stuart said cheerfully.
"Haha, I think you are right. I love our job."
"Me too!" Stuart replied, trying his hardest to hold back the tears.

「喂，他快死了，幫幫忙好嗎？」Rick 懇求著。

我們強擠著笑臉。

「Stuart，你昨晚做了甚麼？」我問。
「我昨晚跟家人一起，很開心啊！」他笑著回答。
「那很好啊，我也跟家人玩得很開心呢！」
「幹！他真的快不行了……」Rick 驚慌地說。
「閉嘴！」我命令道：「玩得開心點！」
「哈哈哈，我很愛這裡啊！喂，你知道嗎，我下班要去騎馬啦！」我哈哈地笑著說。
「哇，那真的很有趣喔，我要……」Stuart 開口時，機關槍的聲音打斷了我們的對話。

子彈瞬速降落在 Rick 身上，然後 Rick 就倒在那個傷者上面。

「Rick 的屍體要把那個男人壓死了。」Stuart 呵呵地說。
「哈哈，你說的沒錯啊！我很愛這份工作。」
「我也是啊！」Stuart 回答時強忍著淚。

It's Just a Prank, Bro

The YouTube community is pretty tight–knit, even though we occasionally plan to trash each other on our respective channels. It's part of the act. I hate having to break it to the much smaller channels that the animosity is staged.

All publicity is good publicity.

Especially, when it's the views that add up to real time money. It doesn't matter that you're writing large paragraphs telling me what I'm doing wrong, because I'll barely ever read it, and when I do, the taste of sweet champagne often masks the bitter taste it leaves in my mouth.

All of us pranking channels started small, but eventually, we had to up our game. We went to limits where the media started criticizing us, "That's sexual harassment." "That's racial discrimination."

The view count rate rose higher. So did our goals.

A week ago today, we got a text from a more popular YouTuber, who asked us, that all fifteen of us could stage, the ultimate prank ever, this April Fool's day. Naturally, collaborations are where our views peak, so all of us agreed. We had to meet at an [undisclosed] location and we would [retracted]. Even though this borders on actual crime, and is

這只是惡作劇好嗎

YouTube 社群是個非常緊密的群體，雖然我們偶爾會計劃在我們各自的頻道上互相排斥，但那只是裝出來的。我很討厭這種假裝充滿強烈敵意、故意把頻道弄得四分五裂的行為。

所有能引起關注的宣傳都是好宣傳。

尤是當觀看次數可以變成真實金錢時，這句話更是貼切。就算你寫一大段字告訴我我做了甚麼錯事也好，我也幾乎不會讀它。但當我真的去讀的時候，總是甜多於苦。

我們這些惡作劇頻道最初都是小規模製作，但最後我們還是把惡作劇升級了。我們開始觸及媒體的底線，他們批評我們說「那是性騷擾」、「那是種族歧視」諸如此類。

隨著觀看次數節節上升，我們的目標也跟著提高了。

一個星期前的今天，我們收到了一個比我們受歡迎的 YouTuber 的訊息，他邀請我們十五人在今年愚人節當天做一個終極惡作劇。理所當然地，合作影片能助我們的觀看次數再創高峰，所以我們全部人都同意了。我們會在[已隱藏]的地點見面，然後我們會[已撤銷]。即使那是幾乎違法的踩界行為，而且比我們做過的節目更瘋狂，但我們還是會做的，反正也只是一個惡作劇。

a far higher leap than any of us have actually taken, we'd do it. It's just a prank, anyway.

When we got to the location today, we were very ceremoniously led in through the [undisclosed] until we got to the hall, where on each side were the weapons stacked for our prank. The walls seemed to be made of thick soundproof material, to prevent the noises from getting out. But the subjects of our pranks seemed absent. Only after the lights dimmed, did we notice the [popular YouTuber]'s head in a case among the displays on the side of the room.

A loud booming voice over the intercom announced the starting of the prank, and how it was us vs us. We'd be live-streamed, and only one of us would make it out. A laughter followed by a chilling remark at the end, how only one of us would be a YouTube legend. We'd all be allowed to live-stream everything, but that's all we could do. No phone calls, no text messages.

I leave this comment here, hoping somebody somewhere reads it. I thought it would all end differently, because it was April Fool's day, and at the end, someone would come and tell us, it was just a prank, none of it was real.

But even as I crouch here, hiding behind a display, the

當我們今天到了那個地方，我們非常榮幸地通過［已隱藏］，然後到達大廳，每一邊都堆放著為惡作劇而準備的武器，牆壁應該是用厚厚的隔音材料製成，以免噪音傳到外面。但被我們惡整的對象似乎不在呢。當燈光逐漸昏暗之後，我們才發現［那個人氣 YouTuber］的頭被放在房間側面展示架的一個箱子裡。

對講機傳來響亮的聲音，宣布惡作劇正式開始，而且這是一場自相殘殺的對決。我們的對決將會在 YouTube 直播，只有一個人能夠勝出。廣播傳來一陣笑聲，然後冷靜地說著，我們當中只有一個人可以成為 YouTube 傳奇人物。我們可以任意直播，但除此之外就甚麼都不能做了，不能通電話，不能發短訊。

我在這裡寫下這個留言，希望有人會看到。我以為這一切都會有個反高潮的結局，因為是愚人節嘛，最後應該會有人來告訴我們，這只是一個惡作劇，所有東西都是假的。

但是，即使我蹲在這裡，躲在一個展示架後面，我也能聽見人們被毆成肉醬的聲音，怎樣聽也不像人造或是預錄的聲音。

我聽見「叮」一聲，因為我現在打開這個網站觸犯了規則，

crunching and snapping sound of people's insides being beaten to a pulp doesn't seem artificial or pre–recorded.

I hear a ding. My location is being given away as I broke the rule simply by opening this website.

Shane walks up to me dragging a blooded claw hammer. He has tears in his eyes, but no emotions.

I wish I could tell you this was just a prank.

所以我的位置被公開了。

Shane 拖著染血的釘錘向著我走過來。他含著淚，但毫無半點感情可言。

我真希望我能告訴你這只是個惡作劇。

The Apocalypse
末 日 啟 示

Do You Look Sufficient Enough for Departure?

In this day and age, we as a species have become infatuated with appearance. Your reputation and love life hinge on whether or not you look like a bombshell model or like you walked out of the pages of Cosmopolitan. Sure, there's going to be that rare flower who'll like you for your personality, but it's highly unlikely that you'll ever meet one of those people in this charlatan–esque society. Romance is dead, but fake beauty is still very much alive, with plastic surgery and makeup pulling in a large amount of revenue.

That and the creators of the system.

It's called a Vanity–Checker AI. The system is installed in your door, and by 2031, it was mandatory for everyone to have one installed in the front door of your home. It basically works like this: you get ready for the day, and you prepare to make your exit. The Vanity–Checker will scan your entire body, and judge for itself if you look presentable enough to leave your home. If you meet the standards, the door will unlock and you'll go about your day.

However, if you don't, it will tell you, "You do not look sufficient enough for departure," and will refuse to let you leave until you look nice. It will offer you suggestions as to why you need to get fixed up, and it could be something as simple as combing a flyaway hair back into place, or putting

你看起來能滿足外出要求嗎？

在這個時代，我們人類已經對外表變得非常迷戀了。你的聲譽和愛情運都會取決於你看起來是否像一個性感模特兒，或者像從著名時尚雜誌走出來那般迷人。當然，還是會有些稀有品種會因為你的個性而喜歡你，但是在這個騙子橫行的社會中，幾乎不可能遇見這種人。浪漫已經不復存在，但假的美女仍然大有人在，而整容醫院和化妝品公司更是利盈豐收。

還有那個系統的創造者。

它叫做「虛榮心檢測器 AI」。這個系統會安裝在你的門上，到了 2031 年，每個人都必須在家的前門安裝這個系統。它基本上是這樣運作的：你辦妥了一切，準備出門的時候，虛榮心檢測器就會掃描你整個身體，它會判斷你看起來夠不夠體面。如果你符合標準，門就會解鎖，你就可以外出了。

但是，如果你不符合標準，它就會告訴你：「你看起來不能滿足外出要求」，並拒絕讓你離開，直到你變得好看為止。它會為你提供建議，來解釋為甚麼你需要修整一下，那可以是簡單的將翹起的頭髮梳好，或穿上一件不同的襯衫去配搭那些褲子。我曾經幾次因為這些愚蠢的建議，使我上班遲到。

on a different shirt to go with those pants. I've been late to work several times for stupid reasons because of this.

And sure, you'd think, "Why not just leave through the back door?" And I would. I really would, except, the Vanity–Checker has complete control over all external doors, as well as windows. It will hack into the Curtains–System for your windows, if it gets to that point, to prevent anyone from seeing you so unsightly. No way out until you look prim and proper for the day.

But the Vanity–Checker wasn't built for security. You leave your door unlocked and anyone can get in, and it's not as if this country has gotten any less violent. The Vanity–Checker did nothing as that psycho got into my house and hacked up my face. And after he was done cleaning himself off, all he had to do was flash a quick smile and it let him back out into the night. It won't let me leave, though; my bloodied, cut up face is too ugly. That maniac stabbed me in the abdomen, too, and I begged the Vanity–Checker to let me out, or at least call an ambulance.

But it wasn't built for that, either.

是的，你會想：「為甚麼不從後門離開？」我會的，我真的會，不過，虛榮心檢測器可以完全控制所有門，連窗戶也是。如果遇到這個情況，它會駭入窗戶的窗簾系統，以防止其他人看到你這麼難看。除非你穿得整潔而又適宜外出，否則沒有其他辦法離開。

但是虛榮心檢測器並不是為了保安理由而設。如果你外出時沒有鎖門，任何人都可以進來。但這並不是因為國家暴力減少而變得安全了，而當那個瘋子走進我的屋子，砍掉我的臉，虛榮心檢測器甚麼也沒有做。在他清理好自己之後，他只需要快速地笑一個，檢測器就讓他溜到夜裡，逃之夭夭。

但它不讓我離開，因為我那血淋淋、被割傷的臉太醜了。那個瘋子也刺傷了我的腹部，我哀求虛榮心檢測器讓我出去，或者至少打電話叫救護車。

但是，它也不是為此而設的。

The Last Man on Earth

I spoke to the Devil today. He was dressed in a blue suit, and his face was young and handsome. He didn't come from hell though, he came down from heaven. I asked him about that.

"I had to talk to God. He can't come to Hell, and he doesn't come down here anymore either, so I had to go to him."

I look around the city, it was completely empty. Cars, belonging to people who thought that today would be like any other, littered the streets. To be fair it was, until everyone suddenly disappeared, everyone but me.

"Did you do this?" I asked.
"We both did," he replied, "Me and God."
"Why wasn't I taken with everyone else?"
"Because there's no room. God and I have tried to fit as many souls as we could into our respective domains but in the end it just wasn't enough."
"What's that mean?"
"It means that unfortunately you'll be staying here. Forever."

As he talked I noticed an odd sound coming from a ways behind us. The Devil continued, not noticing my mild distraction.

地球上最後的人

今天我跟魔鬼說過話。他穿著藍色西裝，臉蛋年輕又帥氣。不過他不是來自地獄，他是從天堂下來的。因為我問過他。

「我不得不和上帝聊一下。祂不能來地獄，也不會再下來這裡了，所以我不得不去找祂。」

我環顧城市，現在像個空城一樣。車子的主人本來以為今天也會像平常的日子般，可是現在那些車子像垃圾般散落街上。公平地說，那是因為所有人都突然消失了，除了我之外。

「是不是你做的？」我問。
「是我們倆做的，」他回答說：「我和上帝」。
「為甚麼我沒有跟其他人一樣被帶走？」
「因為已經沒有位置了，上帝和我已經盡可能將所有靈魂都納入我們各自的領域，但最後還是不夠。」
「那是甚麼意思？」
「這意味著很不幸地，你將會留在這裡，直到永遠。」

他說話的時候，我聽見有些奇怪的聲音從我們背後傳過來。惡魔繼續說話，沒有注意到我恍神了。

"....remember just because you're immortal now doesn't mean you can't get hurt."
"But why? Can't you or God take away my ability to feel pain?"
"Absolutely not; pain and suffering are integral parts of the human experience. God and I may disagree on a lot of things, but we agree on that."

The sound I heard before was getting louder. It sounded like some mad beast, but that was impossible. All the animals had died at the exact moment everyone had disappeared.

"Please," I begged, "There must be something ...."
"This isn't easy for him, you know," he said, "We talked for ages, trying to find a way to save you. He even let me come back home, he would never do that if he wasn't desperate."

The sound I heard was joined by another opposite to it. The Devil must have noticed too because he shoots a sad look in the direction of the sounds before continuing.

"He wanted you to know that he still loves you." he said.
"If he loves me why won't he save me?"
The Devil shook his head "You don't know how lucky you are. God still loves you, but he hates me, his own son. He can't save you and for that, he's sorry. But I have damned you

「……記住現在你是永生的，但不代表你不會受傷。」
「但為甚麼？你或上帝不能幫我弄走感到痛苦的能力嗎？」
「絕對不能。痛苦和苦難是由人類的經驗所組成。上帝和我可能很少達成共識，但我們都同意這一點。」

之前聽到的奇怪聲音現在愈來愈大聲了，聽起來像一些瘋狂的野獸，但那是不可能的，因為每個人消失的時候，所有動物也都同時死掉了。

「拜託……」我哀求：「一定有其他……」
「這對他來說不容易，你知道嗎，」他說：「我們聊了很長時間，嘗試找方法來拯救你。祂甚至讓我回家了，如果祂不是絕望透頂，祂絕對不會這樣做。」

那些聲音現在又在另一邊響起，變成了兩邊都有聲音出現。惡魔也應該注意到了，因為他朝聲音發出的方向擺了個苦臉，才繼續說下去。

「祂希望你知道他還愛著你。」他說。
「如果祂愛我為甚麼不救我？」
魔鬼搖搖頭：「你不知道你是多麼的幸運。上帝仍然愛著你，但祂恨我，他的親兒子。祂不能救你，他為此感到很抱歉。但我已經詛咒了你，我也為此感到很抱歉。」

and for that I'm sorry."

The sounds were all around us now. I could see vague shapes circling us, trying to stay out of view.

"What are those?" I asked.

"What I'm sorry for," he said, "To make room for everyone, or almost everyone, I had to clear the demons and spirits out of hell. They had to go somewhere, so now they're here. They're used to tending to billions of people, but now they'll have to be content with just you. So once again, I'm sorry and goodbye."

那些聲音現在像是圍著了我們一樣。我看到一些模糊的身影圍繞著我們，但又試著不進入我們的視線之內。

「那些是甚麼東西？」我問。
「那就是我道歉的原因，」他說：「為了給每個人，或是說幾乎每個人，都有他們的位置，我必須把惡魔和幽靈從地獄趕出來。他們得去另一個地方落腳，所以現在他們在這裡。他們平常習慣『照顧』數十億人，但現在他們只會『照顧』你一人。所以再一次，對不起，再見。」

A Brave New World

I watched as the man lying down on the bed awoke.

"I can't see. Where am I?" he asked groggily.
"Why, a hospital of course." I replied, "You were in a coma. Do you remember anything?"
"I do. It felt like I was dreaming."
"Were they good?"
"What?"
"Were they good dreams?"
"No actually. They were terrible nightmares."
"I'm sorry to hear that, because it's only going to get worse."
"I can't move." He said, an edge of panic creeping into his voice.
"Are you at all curious as to know how the world's changed in eighty years."
"Eighty!..."
"Yes eighty, a couple of years after you went into your coma, technology started advancing at a rapid pace."
"My body it... it feels wrong."

"Do you believe in God? I think it had to do with playing God. We wanted what God had. So we made more and more powerful machines that could do more and more powerful things, all the while marveling at our own ever growing intelligence. You never answered me before. Do you believe in God?"

美麗新世界

我看著那個躺在床上的男人醒來。

「我看不見，我在哪裡？」他大聲問道。
「哎呀，當然是在醫院啦。」我回答說：「你昏迷了。你還記得甚麼嗎？」
「記得，感覺我是在做夢般。」
「那它們好嗎？」
「甚麼？」
「那些是好夢嗎？」
「不，那些是可怕的惡夢。」
「我很遺憾聽到這個消息，因為之後只會變得更糟。」
「我不能動。」他的聲漸漸帶著恐慌。
「你會不會好奇，這八十年內世界有著怎麼樣的變化？」
「八十！？」
「沒錯是八十，你陷入昏迷幾年之後，科技發展非常蓬勃。」
「我的身體……感覺很不對勁。」

「你相信上帝嗎？我想這是因為我們想要扮演上帝的角色。我們想要上帝所擁有的東西。所以我們製造更多更強大的機器，可以做更多更強大的事情，同時驚歎於我們自己日益增長的智慧。你還沒有回答過我，你相信上帝嗎？」

"I'm not sure."
"Well we weren't sure about God either, so we decided to make our own. A machine made from the most powerful hardware, with enough intelligence to think and reason."
"Is there something covering my eyes?"
"We'd seen the movies of course, so we'd made it so that it needed a human to operate. When The Intelligent Machine Model 2, or Ozymandias as it goes by now, started making machines of it's own, we made sure that those couldn't be used without humans as well."

I paused for a moment. "I'm sorry, I'm rambling. Your visor's turned off, that's why you can't see."
"Can you turn it on for me?"
"I can, but you won't like what you see."
"Please."

I turned on his visor before continuing, "But in our haste to emulate God, we replicated his biggest mistake."

As soon as his visor booted up, he started to scream.

I continued. "The things you create never do what you want them to do."

「我不太肯定。」

「我們也對上帝不太肯定，所以我們決定自己造出來。一台由最強大硬件製成的機器，具有足夠的智慧來思考和推理。」

「是不是有甚麼東西蓋著我的眼睛？」

「我們當然有看過那些電影，所以我們把它弄成需要人類操作的模式。當智能機2號，或現在號稱擁有地球上最高智商、能發揮超乎人類極限能力的智謀者，開始製造自己的機器時，我們得確保它們不能在沒有人類的情況下使用。」

我停頓了一下再說：「很抱歉我說了不著邊際的話。你的面罩已經關上了，所以你看不見。」

「你可以幫我打開它嗎？」

「可以，但你不會喜歡你所看到的。」

「麻煩你了。」

我開啟了他的面罩，然後說：「但我們太急於想要成為上帝，我們複製了他最大的錯誤。」

當他的面罩開啟了之後，他開始尖叫。

我繼續說：「你創造的東西永遠不會如你所願。」

Out of his body jutted slabs of metal, along with clear pipes and multicolored wiring. He started crying. "Have I died? Is this hell or am I still dreaming?"

"I'm afraid you're wide awake."

The machine he's attached to suddenly pulls his body up and starts to walk out of the room. He cries out in pain. It always hurts the first time a machine wears you. "You're to work in the mines. The materials gathered will be used to expand Ozymandias. The machine will move your body so you don't have to worry about figuring out what to do. I wouldn't fight it, it will only hurt."

The machine took him out the door.

"One last thing," I said to the back of his retreating form, "You mentioned dying before. Well thanks to the research of Ozymandias, if you do end up dying, we can just bring you back."

大大小小的金屬板從他的身體穿了出來，連帶著很多透明管子和色彩斑斕的電線。他開始哭了：「我死了嗎？這是地獄嗎？還是我還在做夢？」

「我想你已經很清醒了。」

他依附著的機器突然拉起身子，開始走出房間。他痛得哭了起來。機器第一次穿起你的時候總是會那麼痛苦的了。「你要在礦山工作。收集到的材料將會作擴大智謀者之用。機器會移動你的身體，所以你不用擔心不知道該做甚麼。勸你不要嘗試與它角力，受傷的只有你自己。」

然後機器把他帶了出門。

「最後一件事，」我對著他逐漸遠去的身影說：「你剛才提及過死亡吧？感謝你對智謀者研究的貢獻，如果你最後死了，我們還是可以把你帶回來。」

A Deal with the Devil

The deal was simple, we'd get to ask him a couple of questions and he got to ask us a couple of questions. A bit odd if you ask me. What could The Devil possibly want to know from us? I couldn't tell you.

"Is heaven real?" I asked.
"Yes," he replied, his voice like dying embers in a fireplace, "and so is hell."
"Who goes to heaven?"
"Whoever God wants there."
"I'm afraid that's much too vague for us."
"What's that like?" he asked, his eyes perking up.
"I'm sorry?"
"What's it like to be afraid?"

A bit confused, I tried my best to describe the feeling of fear. My explanation was a bit clumsy but he appeared to be satisfied with it.

"Why'd you want to know that?" I asked.
"Because when God made me, he didn't give me the ability to feel fear. I can't feel lots of things."
"What can you feel?"
"Pain."

I got us back on track.

與惡魔對話

交談很簡單，我們問他幾個問題，他也會問我們幾個問題。老實說也挺奇怪的，惡魔會問我們甚麼呢？我也不知道。

「天堂是真的嗎？」我問道。
「是的，」他的聲音像極了在壁爐裡的餘燼：「地獄也是。」
「誰可以上天堂？」
「上帝想誰上天堂，誰就可以上天堂了。」
「我恐怕這個答案太含糊了。」
「那是怎樣的感覺？」他瞪大眼睛問道。
「你說甚麼？」
「害怕是怎樣的感覺？」

我不知道怎麼回答，唯有盡力描述恐懼的感覺。我的解釋有點笨拙，但他似乎也很滿意。

「為甚麼你會想知道害怕的感覺？」我問。
「因為上帝創造我的時候沒有給我感受害怕的能力，很多東西我都感受不到。」
「那你可以感受到甚麼？」
「痛苦。」

我把話題帶回正軌了。

"Can you elaborate on your answer from before? About heaven?"

"Of course. Heaven is open to all of God's creations, whatever they do."

I breathed a sigh of relief. When I was called in, the people in charge told me that my primary objective was to secure information on how humanity could get to heaven. With that sorted, anything else I gathered was a bonus.

"Are you going to heaven too? Since you were created by God," I asked.

"I could, but I won't," he replied.

"Why?"

"Because I committed the most egregious sin. I did something only God was supposed to do."

"What's that?"

"I tried to create angels. They didn't work out. My angels were made in my image, so I guess I'm to blame. All they do is cause suffering and destruction, so God said they had to go to hell, to suffer for an eternity."

"You mean the demons?"

"Yes, I guess I do. I couldn't go to heaven, not while my creations were suffering. So I decided that when the time came, I would travel to hell and suffer with them."

"Why?"

「你可以再詳細說明一下之前的答案嗎？關於天堂那個。」
「好啊，無論他們做過甚麼，只要是上帝的創造物就可以進入天堂。」

我鬆了一口氣。當初我被委派進行訪問時，負責人告訴我，這次目的主要是設法得到有關人類如何上天堂的方法。根據這個說法，我收集到的其他資料就會是額外的獎勵。

「所以你也可以上天堂嗎？你也是上帝的創造物啊！」
「可以，但我不會。」
「為甚麼？」
「因為我犯下了最惡劣的罪，我做了只有上帝才可以做的事。」
「那是甚麼事？」
「我試過創造天使，但失敗了，我的天使是根據我的形象造出來的，所以我想這是我的錯。他們只會製造痛苦和破壞，所以上帝說他們只能去地獄，永遠受苦。」
「你是指那些惡魔嗎？」
「是的，我想是吧。我不能上天堂，不能在我的創造物正在受苦時上天堂。所以我決定了，當時間到了，我會到地獄與他們一起受苦。」
「為甚麼？」

"Because I love them."

I checked my watch, "Time's almost up."

"Yes it is." he replied.

"I have to go back and get debriefed." I said, preparing to leave the facility. "They'll be ecstatic when they get the good news."

"And what might that be?"

"That no matter what we do, we're going to heaven."

"But you're not, or anyone else for that matter."

"But," I said, my voice wavering, "You said…"

"Yes, I know what I said my child. But you're not one of God's creations," he said with a tone I would mistake for sadness if I didn't know better,

"You're one of mine."

「因為我愛他們。」

我看一看錶：「時間差不多了。」

「是的。」他回答。

「我要回去跟他們匯報了。」我邊說邊準備離開：「如果他們聽到我的好消息，他們肯定超開心。」

「那是甚麼好消息？」

「無論我們做甚麼，我們最後也是會上天堂的。」

「但你不會，就此而言，其他人都不會。」

「但是……」我聲音顫抖著：「你不是說……」

「是的孩子，我知道我說過甚麼。但你不是上帝創造的，」他語氣差點讓我誤以為他很悲傷，但我很清楚他不是。

「你是我造的。」

The Empty

Sally sat on her front porch, casually sipping her iced tea and watching as the Empty waited at the edge of her farm.

No–one knew what caused the Empty to appear, or why. All anyone could tell, it has just popped up in some tiny town called Harmony. Probably why no one noticed right away. At the time, it was just a small mass of pitch black nothingness, about the size of a tire. It was a big deal at the time, with all the eggheads and boffins coming down to poke and prod it. Turns out that if something goes into the Empty, it doesn't come out. It just simply ceases to be. Doesn't matter how strong it is, or how durable, or even how big, the Empty consumed it all.

Then those people noticed that it was growing. About five miles a day, more or less. And that's when everyone got really scared. In one day, it consumed Harmony and the surrounding area, along with all those nosy scientists. Some people think they activated it or fed it, but who really knows?

And now Sally's farm, a farm that she had gotten from her dad, who got it from his dad, was about to be consumed within the day. The old barn where she'd milked the cows. The fields where she'd run and play when she was a kid. The house she'd grown up in all her life. All would be consigned unto oblivion by sundown.

虛無

Sally 坐在前廊，隨意地喝著冰茶，看著「虛無」在她的農場邊緣等待著。

沒有人知道甚麼導致「虛無」出現，或是它為甚麼會出現。但所有人都知道，它在一個叫做 Harmony 的小鎮上出現。或者因為這樣所以沒有人立即注意到。那時候它還只是一小塊像輪胎般大的黑色虛無。當時居民覺得是一件大事，所有的書呆子和科學家都走過去戳一下、捅一下。發現如果有東西進入了「虛無」，它就不會再出來，就這樣消失了。無論它有多堅固、多耐用，甚至多大，「虛無」都會把它們吞噬了。

然後那些人注意到它正在增長，每天大約擴大五英里。自那時開始，每個人都嚇壞了。一天之內，它吞噬了 Harmony 和周邊的地區，連那些多管閒事的科學家也吞掉了。有些人認為是因為他們激活了它或餵飼了它，但又有誰知道真相呢？

而 Sally 的那個農場，是她父親留下來的，也是她父親的父親留下來的，但這裡很快就會被吞噬了。Sally 小時候會在畜棚裡幫母牛擠牛奶、在田裡跑跳遊玩著、在這間房子裡經歷了一切事物。而這一切都會在日落後化為烏有。

Sally knew that she should have evacuated by now, moved as far away from the Empty as she could. But what was the point? Nobody could stop the Empty from growing. Nobody could even explain what it was, since all attempts to even analyze the thing ended in failure. It would be slow, but the Empty would eventually spread over the earth.

Of course, some people suggested that they should evacuate to space, like in the movies. But that was a pipe dream at best. Humanity couldn't be asked to field enough ships to evacuate a viable population into space. And even if they could, The Empty was growing up as well as out. It would probably consume anything in orbit. It would just take a lot longer.

In the end, the choice was simple. She could join the fleeing population, eventually being corralled into a mass of panicked humanity as oblivion consumed them all bit by bit. Or she could simply wait, surrounded by her favorite things in her own home, and go out on her own terms.

It really wasn't that hard a decision.

And as the Empty crept, slowly but surely, onto her farm, she took another sip of her tea. She noticed the pitcher was empty. But that was alright. Sally figured she had time to make one more batch.

Sally 知道她其實可以現在就離開這裡，盡可能地遠離「虛無」。但又有甚麼意思呢？沒有人可以阻止「虛無」的成長，甚至沒有人可以解釋那是甚麼，無論嘗試分析這件事多少次也好，最後都是失敗告終。雖然速度緩慢，但「虛無」最終還是會蔓延到整個地球。

理所當然地，有人建議他們應該撤離到太空，就像在電影裡看到的一樣。但那只會是個空想，不可能會有足夠的太空船把有生育能力的人類撤離到太空。即使有足夠的位置，「虛無」也可以向外蔓延，它可能會吞噬在星球軌道上的所有東西，那只是需要更長的時間。

來到最後，只有兩個選擇。她可以和其他人一起逃離，然後最終與他們一起陷入恐慌，因為「虛無」正在一點一點地蠶食著他們。或者她可以繼續等待，身處自己家中，被最喜愛的事物包圍，然後接受自己大限將至。

那真的不難下決定。

「虛無」正在蔓延著，慢慢地但肯定地，會蔓延到她的農場，Sally 又喝了一口茶。她注意到茶壺已經空了。但是沒關係，她仍然有時間多沏一壺茶。

We Could Do Nothing But Lie Down

I remember the day the spider–like creatures swarmed out of their holes and covered the moon's surface. NASA telescopes captured high definition video of the masses of creatures, throbbing and heaving as far as the eye could see. They were as big as cars and I nearly lost my mind when I caught a glimpse of them on the news.

I remember the ensuing months as humanity reacted to the presence of new life in our solar system. Many wanted to nuke the lunar surface until it was glass. Others wanted to make peace. Some worshiped them as gods. Personally, whenever I looked up at the moon, brownish red with the skittering bodies of monsters, I could barely stop myself from shaking.

I remember when CNN broke footage of the creatures building massive ships on the surface. They were intelligent. This was enough to cause near panic. They were coming to us.

I remember the day they sent their first message. The sound was harsh and guttural and interspersed with a horrible clicking. Top linguists around the world were called in to translate.

我們只能躺著

我記得那些像蜘蛛般的生物從牠們的洞裡湧出來，並覆蓋了月球表面的那天。美國太空總署的望遠鏡以高清拍攝著月球表面，畫面拍到無窮無盡的生物在跳動、搖晃著。它們的大小跟汽車差不多，當我在新聞看到它們的消息時，我幾乎發瘋了。

我記得接下來的幾個月，當人類知道太陽系有新生物跡象時的反應。很多人想以核武攻擊月球表面來消除那些怪物；其他人想要跟它們和解；有些人則視它們為神明，崇拜著它們。而我呢，每當我抬頭看著月亮，看到那些棕紅色的怪物滿地亂走，我都會不住發抖。

我記得 CNN 播放了那些怪物在月球表面上搭建了很多巨型太空船的鏡頭。它們是有智慧的生物，單是這點已經足以引起恐慌。它們要來找我們了。

我記得他們發出第一個訊息的那天。那個聲音是很刺耳的喉音，當中又夾雜著可怕的咔噠咔噠聲，世界各地的頂尖語言學家都被召來進行翻譯工作。

I remember two weeks later when the brownish red tint of the moon gave way to the milky white we had almost forgotten as the monsters entered into their ships. Earth was on high alert, all nations' armies prepared for assault. And then the ships took off and left in the opposite direction.

And I remember the next day, when the linguists finally decoded the strange message and played it for the whole world to hear: "If you value your lives, run."

我記得兩個星期後，月亮由棕紅色變回了乳白色，我們幾乎忘記了怪物已經上了太空船。地球所有人都高度戒備，各國軍隊都在備戰狀態，準備進行攻擊。然而那些太空船向著地球的相反方向起飛離開了。

然後我記得那天之後，那些語言學家終於成功解讀了那個奇怪的訊息，並將它播放給整個世界：「如果你們不想死，就快點跑吧。」

The Face of God

Two very important things happened in the year 2075, the first was that humanity discovered a way to get to heaven, and the second was the apocalypse.

It turns out that on Pluto there is a region of immensely strong gravity. Strong enough that light shouldn't have been able to escape it. But from that place on Pluto, a bright, pure light shone. It's how we found it in the first place. Pluto's too far away to see it with the naked eye, but even in daylight, everyone could see that light.

Now the apocalypse was an entirely different matter. That came from under the earth and oceans. Tall creatures with smooth carapaces, and black unblinking eyes. They stood upright, but when they moved they skittered around on the ground like cockroaches. They were quick and their exoskeletons were tough, they were strong enough to tear an average human male in half and no matter how many the army killed, there would always be more to take their place.

Countries were already planning manned expeditions to investigate the anomaly on Pluto, but with the appearance of these creatures an expedition was fast tracked. I was one of the few priests chosen to accompany the astronauts on their interstellar journey to heaven. My official role was to provide morale support for the crew, but I think we all knew us priests

上帝的臉

2075 年發生了兩件大事，第一件事是人類發現了上天堂的方法，第二件事是世界末日。

原來，在冥王星上有一個引力非常強大的區域，強得令光都不能逃脫。但是在那個地方有一個既明亮又清澈的發光地帶，我們最初就是這樣發現它的。冥王星距離地球太遠，用肉眼看不見它，但現在即使是白天，每個人都可以看到那道光。

而世界末日又是另外一件完全相反的事，跟冥王星事件不同，這次在地底和海底發生。那些高大的生物有著光滑外殼和不眨動的黑色眼睛。他們正正地站著，但是當他們移動時，就會像蟑螂般在地上飛掠而過。他們速度很快，而且有著堅硬的外殼，強大得可以將人類男性撕開一半，而且無論他們那邊死了多少「人」也好，總是會有更多的「人」來填補他們的位置。

各國本身正在計劃派出太空探險隊來調查冥王星的異常情況，但隨著這些生物的出現，探險隊需要馬上出征。我是少數被選中的牧師之一，負責陪伴著太空人一起到天堂。我的職務是維持全體人員的士氣，但我想我們都心裡有數，我們這些牧師被派到這裡，某種程度上是想我們説服對方幫助我們。

were being sent to somehow convince whoever was on the other side to help us.

I have been steadfast in my faith, even with the apocalypse. But something I heard before we left keeps bothering me, no matter how hard I try to forget it. It was a quote that went, "I saw the face of God, and it was weeping." I guess it upset me so because I was scared it would be true. What if when I saw God, he was weeping because he couldn't stop what was going on. What if we were already doomed and something stronger than God had us in its power. These thoughts so troubled me that I half hoped our craft would crash, so I wouldn't have to find out for sure. But we made it to Pluto, and we went through to the other side.

On the other side, we saw what could only be described as angels and a being that had to be God. He was immense, like us but unlike us. As we got closer, I saw that he was looking at the earth. I somehow knew he could see everything going on. As I watched him, all my previous worries were replaced by a terrifying realization. Because I saw what he saw, I saw the creatures ripping soldiers not old enough to drink apart, I saw them crush small children's heads like grapes, I saw them dismember entire families. I saw his face as he saw all this.

I saw the face of God, and it was smiling.

就算已是世界末日，我也會一直堅守我的信念。但是，離開地球之前我聽到的一句話，不管我多麼努力地忘記它，還是令我十分困擾。那句話是這樣的：「我看到了上帝的臉，祂在哭。」這令我很心煩，因為我很害怕那是真的。如果我看到上帝在哭是因為他無法阻止正在發生的一切，那該怎麼辦？如果我們已經注定劫數難逃，然後有一些比上帝更強大的東西掌控著人類，那該怎麼辦？這些想法讓我很煩惱，我有時會寧願我們的太空船撞毀算了，那我就不必知道真相了。但是我們還是到了冥王星，然後我們又到了它的另一端。

在另一邊，我們看到應該是天使的東西，還有應該是上帝的生物。祂很龐大，跟我們一樣，但又不太一樣。當我們走近時，我看到他在望著地球。我不知怎的覺得他可以看到地球所發生的一切事情。當我看著他的時候，我之前所有的擔憂已經一掃而空，換來的只有令我嚇壞的領悟。因為我看到他正在看的東西：我看到那些生物正在把軍人們撕成碎片，我看到他們把小孩子的頭當成葡萄般搗爛，看到他們把一個又一個家庭弄得肢離破碎。我看到他望著這一切的臉。

我看到了上帝的臉，祂在笑。

This is the Emergency Broadcast Network

WARNING: We have received reports from NASA describing a strange phenomenon in the upper atmosphere. These reports are similar in description to transcripts provided by the NSA. Until the nature of this phenomenon has been verified, we advise you to stay in your homes for the time being.

WARNING: The Phenomenon has increased in intensity and can now be seen with the naked eye. To prevent any damage to your optical nerves, we advise everyone to lock all windows and refrain from looking up at the sky. When the Phenomenon has been identified, or stops being active, then an all clear message will be given.

WARNING: My god, it's so bright. The sky is...

WARNING: Go outside and look.

WARNING: Thye took you. They took you and you didn't even notcie.

WARNING: What you see above iz a cage, a prisun. A cage we have brokin. When you sent thos men in those primitive machines up ther, it angered them and they sent you imposters back. Thye took you and when they get board, they'll hurt forever.

緊急廣播

警告：我們收到了美國太空總署的報告，記述了大氣層上層的奇怪現象，此等報告與國家安全局提供的文本相似。在未能證實現實屬哪種性質之前，我們建議您們暫時留在家中。

警告：現象強度增加，現在已經可以用肉眼看到。為了防止對您的視覺神經造成任何傷害，我們建議您們鎖起所有窗戶，不要仰望天空。當成功識別現象或當現象停止活動時，我們將會發出警報解除訊息。

警告：我的天啊，太亮了。天空很……

警告：去外面看看。

警告：他門把你帶走了，他們把你帶走了而你刷覺不到。

警告：你可以看到上方有個籠子，那示個監玉，那個籠子是我們破籠兒出的地方。當你把那些坐在原始機器裡的人送去那裡，激怒了他們，所以他們把那些冒充品送回來給你們作回禮。他門到達了就會把你帶走，讓你永遠受苦。

WARNING: They think themselves powerful because they control you. You are beneath them and they are beneath us. So come you unenlightened primitives, come and see the light outside before they brick you in again. Come and see...

WARNING: DO NOT GO OUTSIDE. DO NOT GO OUTSIDE. DO NOT GO OUTSIDE. DO NOT GO OUTSIDE. DO NOT GO OUTSIDE. DO NOT GO OUTSIDE. DO NOT GO OUTSIDE. DO NOT GO OUTSIDE. DO NOT GO OUTSIDE. DO NOT GO OUTSIDE. DO NOT GO OUTSIDE.

WARNING: The Phenomenon has been determined to be errant meteor burning up in the atmosphere. Disregard all messages preceding this one. We apologize if they caused you any distress, they were due to a technical malfunction. Please forgive us, our flesh is weak and prone to mistake. Once again, the Phenomenon is gone, it is safe to go outside. You are safe.

警告：他們認為自己很強大，因為他們控制著你。你在他們之下，而他們在我們之下。所以來吧，未被啟蒙的原始人，在他們把你關進牢裡之前來看看外面的光吧。來看看吧……

警告：不要外出。不要外出。不要外出。不要外出。不要外出。不要外出。不要外出。不要外出。不要外出。不要外出。不要外出。

警告：成功鑑定現象為有隕石在大氣層中燃燒。請忽略此前所有消息。如果對您造成任何困擾，我們深表歉意，剛才是技術故障。請原諒我們，我們的肉體很弱，很容易出錯。重複，現象消失了，可以安全外出了，您安全了。

The End Times

I was the first one to see a falling angel.

I was in my backyard stargazing, when a bright light streaked across the sky and a few moments later Gabriela smashed into my backyard.

She was really tall, I had to use two mattresses for her bed and move out most of the things in my living room to make room for her to sleep. She was very badly injured. Something had taken huge bites out of her chest, her eyes had been ripped out and one of her wings had been torn off. She spent most of her time unconscious and the rest gibbering in an unknown tongue.

She only spoke to me twice, once to tell me her name and the other time was to respond to a question I had asked her. "How did you get injured Gabriela?" I had asked. "War" she replied. She died a few hours after that.

In the following days, more and more angels fell from the sky. These angels however, were already dead, their bodies had been mutilated, sometimes so badly, that if not for their height and wings, we wouldn't know for sure if they were angels. Surprisingly, while many people panicked, peace as a whole was kept and it only took a few days before the buses and trains were running on time again.

末日降臨

我是第一個看到天使從天而降的人。

當時我在後院觀星，突然一道明亮的光線劃過天空，不一會兒 Gabriela 就墜落在我的後園。

她很高很高，我要用兩張床墊來做她的床，還要把客廳大部分的東西都移走，她才有位置睡覺。她傷得很重，胸腔位置被大口大口地咬傷了，雙眼被挖走了，其中一隻翅膀也被撕掉了。她大部分時間都是沒有意識的，其餘時間則是口齒不清地呢喃著，不過我也聽不懂那種語言。

她只對我說過兩次話，一次是告訴我她的名字，另一次是回答我的問題：「Gabriela，你是怎樣受傷的？」「戰爭。」她回答。她在幾個小時後就身亡了。

接下來幾天，愈來愈多天使從天上掉下來。不過這些天使已經死了，他們都被肢解了，有時候誇張得我只能靠身高和翅膀來判斷他們的身份。出乎意料的是，雖然很多人都驚慌失措，但整個社會大致上都很平靜，公共汽車和火車只花了幾天就再次正常運作。

When the rain of corpses from heaven stopped, people were overjoyed. When huge cracks in the earth started to appear, they were less so. When fire and lava began to bubble up through the cracks, people rushed to monasteries, churches, mosques, and temples, anywhere they thought they might find answers. When the earth rumbled, and the cracks opened to spew out a horde of demons, we finally understood.

You see, the demons were all dead. Their bodies had been mutilated, just like the angels were. I thought that heaven and hell were in a war against one another, but they were actually fighting together. Against something else, something worse.

And it had won.

下了幾天的屍體雨終於停止了，人們都樂不可支。但當地面開始出現巨大的裂縫，他們就不這麼開心了。裂縫裡開始噴出火焰和熔岩，人們紛紛跑到修道院、教堂、清真寺和寺廟，或是其他他們認為會找到答案的地方。地下隆隆作響，裂縫裂得更大了，一大堆惡魔被丟了出來……我們終於明白了。

那些惡魔都已經死了，他們都被肢解了，就像之前的天使一樣。我本以為這是一場天堂與地獄的鬥爭，但他們其實是並肩作戰，一起對抗著另一樣東西，一樣更可怕的東西。

而且它戰勝了。

Survival Rules
生 存 規 則

Constructive Criticism

"Heeellllloooo, my busy little worker bees! This is your C.E.O. Wendy Addams, yet again giving out another progress report! Now that you've entered hour four of this lovely little death match, let's see who'd literally kill for that promotion! Haha–get it?

"Firstly, Anne, creative use of the company–provided staplers! I'm not naming names, but it seems a few individuals just couldn't handle it! Haha!

"And Gregory. Who knew under that soft, nerdy exterior there was a complete monster? You sure cleared out floor three, didn't you, Gregory? Those assholes in the Engineering Sector won't be bothering you anymore, that's for sure!

"While we're on about engineering, I've noticed that while Tom's odd little contraption made from the printer did do the trick for a while, he was no match for Tammy's gun. Sorry, Tom. I'd tell you what you did wrong, but you're dead!

"Props to Tammy for finding the hidden armory, but Tammy–dear, your aim could be better. Tom suffered for exactly six minutes, two seconds because you didn't get the quick headshot you were hoping for. One tip, Tammy: Aim slightly above your target if you can't achieve point–blank. Good luck with that!

建設性批評

「大一家一好一親愛的忙碌小工蜂！我是你的C.E.O. Wendy Addams，再次發出另一個進度報告！現在你已經進入這個可愛死亡小比賽的第四個小時，讓我們看看誰會為了升職『人擋殺人，佛擋殺佛』吧！哈哈，懂我意思嗎？

「首先，Anne，很有創意地使用公司提供的釘書機！我不指名道姓説是誰了，但似乎有幾個人招架不住了呢！哈哈！

「還有Gregory，誰知道這個溫柔的書呆子，內裡原來是頭不折不扣的怪物？Gregory你把三樓清理掉了，對嗎？那些工程部的混蛋肯定不會再騷擾你了！

「説起工程，我有看到Tom在打印機那邊弄了個怪怪的小裝置，雖然是成功保衛了一陣子，但還是鬥不過Tammy的槍呢。對不起呢，Tom。我很想告訴你你做錯了甚麼，但你已經死了！

「我在此向Tammy致敬，找到隱藏的軍械庫實在不容易呢。但是親愛的Tammy，你可以瞄得更準呢。因為你做不到預期的快速爆頭，使Tom受了足足六分鐘零兩秒的痛苦。Tammy，給你一個提示吧，如果你直接瞄準目標時射失的話，就瞄準略高於目標的位置吧。祝你好運！

"Now, Jeremy, Jeremy, Jeremy. Those hours at the gym paid off, didn't they? One thing: be a little more forceful, will you? Excellent use of company fire extinguishers. However, optimum killing momentum allows for just one impact to kill. This saves precious energy on your part. Remember our company motto, and 'Be efficient,' Jeremy!

"Ah. Feeling tired, Sharon? Maybe pick up a snack in the cafeteria. Or not. Jason's guarding the fridge.

"Oooh, sorry, Jason! I just gave away your position, didn't I? Why couldn't you be more clever like Harriet, who's hiding in the basement?

"Whoops."

"Ahem. Um, Nancy, the way you took out that intern was EPIC! Can't clean up his own mess, poor thing, after cleaning up all of ours. But the bitch probably deserves it. Perhaps the next intern will know the difference between decaf–mocha and decaf–java. Honestly.

"Now, pay attention, my little worker bees! Our population has been reduced from six–hundred to two–seventy five, with approximately forty–three being due to suicide. Shameful, right? Those forty–three do not properly represent this

「好吧，Jeremy，Jeremy，Jeremy。在健身房鍛煉了那麼久，現在有回報了吧？但是，要再更用力一點，可以嗎？有好好善用公司的滅火筒呢。不過，最佳殺戮動量只需一次衝擊就足以致命，這可以讓你節省你寶貴的精力喔。Jeremy，請你記住我們公司的座右銘：『要有效率』！

「啊，Sharon，你累了嗎？去食堂拿點小吃吧。喔不，Jason 正守著冰箱。

「噢噢噢，對不起，Jason！我是不是透露了你的位置呢？你為甚麼不像聰明的 Harriet 躲在地下室呢？

「哎呦。」

「咳咳，唔，Nancy，你幹掉那個實習生的手法簡直是經典！那可憐的孩子幫我們收拾好一切，卻不能收拾自己的爛攤子。但是那個婊子可能是活該吧。也許下一個實習生會知道無咖啡因摩卡和無咖啡因咖啡的分別吧，拜託。

「好的，我的小工蜂，請注意！我們的人口已經從六百減少到二百七十五，當中約有四十三人是因為自殺而身亡。真可恥，對吧？那四十三個人不能恰當地代表這家公司。請謹記要做．個．好．榜．樣。還有不要忘記我們的另一個

company. Be. Sure. You. Do. And don't forget our other motto: 'work until death!' That is all!

"Actually, wait, wait, wait, one more thing. A special Congratulations to floor five worker Emerson Jones for his fabulous kill count of one–hundred and forty–seven! Watch out for this guy!

"Oh, duh! Wish Phil and Mark a Happy Birthday! Or… just Mark. That will be all until I give out the progress report for hour five! Keep slaying until then, my little worker bees! This is Wendy Addams, signing out."

座右銘：『鞠躬盡瘁，死而後已』！

「其實呢，等一下，等一下，還有一件事。在此特別祝賀五樓員工 Emerson Jones 的殺戮數已達一百四十七，非常優秀！小心這個傢伙喔！

「噢，呃！祝 Phil 和 Mark 生日快樂！或者……只是 Mark 吧。報告暫時告一段落，我們在第五小時的進度報告再見！繼續殺戮吧，我的小工蜂，我是 Wendy Addams，再見。」

A Memo to Disney Cast Members

A Disney Cast Members' top priority is the comfort and safety of our guests. For this reason, all Disney World employees must follow these rules. Failure to do so will result in disciplinary action.

Ask to examine the photos our guests have taken. Be friendly. Check for abnormalities. If any are found, call for security. Guests may be distracted with free merchandise.

Every seventh photograph taken on the Dinosaur attraction must be deleted. If questioned, explain that it was a technical error and offer Fast Passes.

The rumors of sharks and crocodiles in the Lagoon are false. However, there is no swimming outside of designated swimming pools on Disney property.

Dead alligators are common around the Lagoon. Simply evacuate the area, call security, then take note of how much has been eaten.

There is only one Mickey out at once. If you find a second Mickey having an autograph session, check for eye holes. All Disney costumes have eye holes.

If you don't find eye holes, allow the session to continue, but

致迪士尼藝員的備忘錄

迪士尼演藝人員的首要職責是要確保來賓安全及舒適。因此，所有迪士尼樂園的員工必須遵守以下規則，否則將會受到紀律處分。

請檢查來賓所拍的照片，保持友善的態度，並檢查有否異常。如有異常，請通知保安人員。可以用免費商品分散來賓注意力。

在恐龍園區拍的第七張照片，每張都要刪除掉，如有來賓詢問因由，可解釋是技術錯誤，然後派發快證給他們。

瀉湖裡鯊魚和鱷魚的傳說是假的，然而，除了迪士尼樂園物業的指定泳池外，其餘地方不准游泳。

在瀉湖內發現死掉的短吻鱷是很常見的事，只要疏散該區域，通知保安人員，以及紀錄吃了多少則可。

每次只可有一隻米奇出現，如發現有第二隻米奇出現在簽名環節，請檢查它是否有眼孔。所有迪士尼的戲服都有眼孔。

如發現沒有眼孔，可讓環節繼續進行，但不准來賓拍照。在該環節結束後請馬上通知保安。

disallow photos. Call security immediately after the session concludes.

If you spot a second Mickey off to the side, lure him into the tunnels. That's what the ducks are there for. Leave immediately afterwards, and do not look back.

The Disney World security unit does not wear specially marked clothing. If you see someone wearing a shirt that says "Disney Security", shut down that section of the park immediately.

Following these rules will help ensure a safe and pleasurable trip to the happiest place on Earth.

So stay knowledgeable, and stay safe.

如在旁發現第二隻米奇，請引誘它進入隧道。那裡的鴨子就是為了這而存在。之後請立即離開，不要回頭看。

迪士尼樂園的保安人員並不會穿著有特殊標記的衣物，如看見有人穿著「迪士尼保安」字眼的上衣，應立刻關閉該園區。

為了確保來賓在這個地球上最歡樂的地方，可以享受到安全又心曠神怡的旅程，員工請遵守以上指引。

請保持警覺，注意安全。

Claudia Winters' Guide to Surviving the Labyrinth House

Rule #1: Remember that the circular windows lead either only out or only in. When departing from the house, never, ever gamble with circular windows. Be safe, and use the square windows, since they're two-way. **Avoid the triangle windows entirely.**

Rule #2: When traversing through the house, it is safer to go through the wall passages. Never go through the rooms without another human with you. The portraits **won't remain still** otherwise.

Rule #3: Find/steal a decent weapon. Always keep it on you.

Rule #4: Never listen to the Residents dine. Seriously, just find a way to plug your ears. Even though they won't look for you when they're dining, the noises that occur… well, you'll wish you hadn't heard them.

Rule #5: If you must fall asleep, find a safe place before doing so, and never sleep for long. You may **not wake up** if you sleep in the wrong place.

Rule #6: When met with a dead end, find the panel that leads to the room, and traverse through rooms carefully. Previous players have carved symbols into the panels that lead back into the walls. It looks like this: ø

迷宮屋生存指南

規則一：記住圓形窗戶只能單向出來或者進去。當離開房子時，千萬不要拿圓形窗戶來冒險。注意安全，並使用方形窗口，因為它們是雙向的。**完全迴避所有三角形窗口**。

規則二：穿過房子時，使用牆壁通道會比較安全。如沒有另一個人跟你一起，不要走過房間。否則，肖像畫**不會保持靜止**。

規則三：查找 / 偷取一個像樣的武器。時刻帶在身上。

規則四：不要聽到居民用餐的聲音。真的不要，找個辦法堵住你的耳朵吧。即使他們用餐時不會找你，但發出的那些聲音……呃，你會希望你從來沒有聽過。

規則五：如果你必須入睡，先找一個安全的地方才睡，而且不要睡太久。如果你睡在錯誤的地方，你可能**不會醒來**。

規則六：遇到死胡同時，查找通往房間的面板，並小心穿過房間。之前的玩家在可以通往牆壁的面板刻了符號，那個符號是這樣的：ø

Rule #7: Find a way to keep track of the time. I don't care how, just do it. The Residents will retire to certain rooms at a particular hour, and if you're in there when they see you... Well, the players they find aren't treated kindly.

Rule #8: If you hear Residents on the other side of the wall you're in(hopefully you kept doing Rule #2 as often as possible), then keep silent, and keep still. You are free to move once you can no longer hear the whispers.

Rule #9: Always move quickly. You're not the only thing crawling around in the walls.

Rule #10: Avoid going to the center of the house. My friend never came back, and you won't either. **Trust me.**

Rule #11: If you encounter the sections of the house where there are **walls of human flesh**, you better be able to use your weapon well. Hopefully you didn't think that pair of scissors you happened upon would do the job. Always keep in mind that **those walls are hungry.**

Rule #12: Don't panic when the house shifts. Just don't fucking panic. It's called Labyrinth House for a reason, it's not supposed to be fucking easy. If you carry on screaming, then you'll be caught by the Residents.

規則七：找個可以知道時間的方法。我不在乎你如何知道時間，總之一定要找到方法。居民會在特定的時間撤退到某些房間，如果你在那裡，然後讓他們看到你……唔……他們不會善待被發現的玩家。

規則八：如果聽見牆另一邊居民的聲音（希望你盡可能遵守規則二），請保持沉默，不要動。當你沒有再聽到低語聲，你就可以自由移動了。

規則九：保持行動迅速。你不是唯一在牆上爬來爬去的東西。

規則十：不要去房子的中間位置。我的朋友沒有再回來，而你也不會倖免。**相信我**。

規則十一：如遇到有**人肉牆**的區域，你最好能好好運用你的武器。希望你不會認為那把偶然發現的剪刀可以幫得上忙。請時刻記住，**那些牆壁很餓**。

規則十二：如遇到房子移位，請不要驚慌。總之千萬不要嚇倒。這裡叫做「迷宮屋」是有原因的，不會這麼容易的。如果你繼續尖叫的話，你就會被居民抓到。

Rule #14: Never attempt to find the missing rule.

Rule #15: **Don't let the Residents catch you. Ever.** They are by far the worst creatures you will ever encounter in the House. Do remember **you are playing their game.** The only way to leave the House is to escape, and there are only two ways to leave the House. You can succeed in making it to the outer wall and exit through a window, with your sanity partially intact, or completely gone, but as for the other option…

Well, you probably ignored Rule #4, didn't you?

規則十四：不要嘗試查找那個缺少了的規則。

規則十五：**不要讓居民抓到你，千萬不要**。他們會是你至今在屋子裡遇過最糟糕的生物。請記住**你是在玩他們的遊戲**。想要離開屋子只有逃走這個方法，而離開屋子也只會有兩種下場：你可以走到外牆，穿過窗口離開，那麼你的理智會在一定程度上完好無缺，或者會完全消失；至於另一個……

唔……你是不是忽略了規則四了呢？

Fifteen Things I've Learned in Fifteen Years of Existing

1. The girls who've made the mistake of wandering into the forest at night refuse to speak of whatever they've seen.

2. Chores are important, especially feeding Heretia. Feeding a giant spider isn't easy, but if Heretia isn't given corpses, an unfortunate feeder is good enough for her.

3. The Elders aren't to be disturbed during virgin sacrifices. Doing so, regardless of the manner, will result in being moved up on the sacrifice list – if you've been marked on there already. If not? Well, you're definitely on there, now.

4. One can make themselves ineligible for sacrifice by relinquishing their purity.

5. Biting off the head of the man you lost your virginity to is difficult, whether you're a descendant of Arachne or not.

6. Heretia accepts any and all corpses, which can be helpful in getting rid of evidence.

7. Harming any kind of spider, in self defense or spite, results in immediate sacrifice. I've lost several sisters that way.

生存十五年來學會的十五件事

1. 那些在夜裡不小心走到樹林裡的女孩都不肯說出她們看到過甚麼。

2. 家務很重要，特別是餵養 Heretia。餵養一隻巨型蜘蛛並不容易，但是如果 Heretia 沒有得到屍體，那個不幸的飼養員對她來說就已經夠好了。

3. 在處女獻祭時，不要騷擾那些長老。否則，無論方式如何，你在犧牲品清單上的排名就會變得更前。如果你不在清單上的話，嗯，你的名字肯定會立即在那裡出現。

4. 可以通過放棄自己的純潔，來使自己不符合犧牲的資格。

5. 無論你是否紡織女阿拉赫的後裔，咬掉那個取了你貞操的男人的頭，都是一件很困難的事。

6. Heretia 接受任何及所有屍體，這有助於毀滅證據。

7. 無論是出於自衛或是有意，傷害任何蜘蛛都會立即犧牲。我已經因此失去了幾個姊妹。

8. The souls of the damned, or rather, those sacrificed, reside in the husks of spider bodies. I found this out when four of them tried to strike up a conversation with me.

9. Heretia's cage is not to be disturbed. Ever. Freeing the focal point of the Order's worship results in immediate banishment to the forest.

10. Bones of people appear at the edge of the forest. Picked clean. The others know it is best not to question why.

11. Hiding fangs can be difficult, or so I've been told. I think it's pretty easy.

12. Not getting to bed quick enough results in being caught up in a swarm of spiders. You're carried through the halls of the cave, screaming during it all, until they retreat in the presence of daylight. The night belongs to the spiders.

13. I've found I envy a spider's talent to an extreme level. I wish I could weave and snare people like I used to.

14. The Elders don't suspect me as much when I do my chores and be a good girl without being told.

8. 那些被詛咒的、或者說是已犧牲的人的靈魂，他們住在蜘蛛的外殼裡。曾經有四個靈魂試著跟我談話，我才發現到的。

9. 不能打擾 Heretia 的籠子，永遠不能。如果釋放命令崇拜的關鍵物，會馬上被流放到森林裡。

10. 森林的邊緣會有人骨出現，骨頭血肉散盡一地。最好不要問為甚麼。

11. 要把毒牙隱藏起來可能很難，我是這樣聽說的，但我覺得挺簡單的。

12. 如果沒有及時上床睡覺的話，會被蜂擁而至的蜘蛛抓到。他們會帶你穿過洞穴的大廳，使你一直尖叫著，直到陽光出現時，他們才會撤退。因為夜晚是屬於蜘蛛的。

13. 我發現自己真的很羨慕蜘蛛的天賦，簡直是羨慕到極點。我也很想可以像以前一樣編網和誘捕人們。

14. 當我有做家務和自動自覺當個乖女孩時，長老們沒有像以前那麼懷疑我。

15. Children of Heretia reside in the woods. Like how a human soul can be stored in a spider's body, my soul is safely tucked in this girl's frame. I do not speak of the woods. My sisters – the wise ones, anyway – say that the plan will be set in motion shortly. The Order will fall.

Mother– your vengeance will be had.

15. Heretia 的孩子住在樹林裡。就像人類的靈魂可以存藏在蜘蛛的身體裡一樣，我的靈魂也安穩地擠進這個女孩的身軀。我不提及森林了，無論如何，我的姐姐，她們都是聰明人，説這個計劃很快就會啟動了，命令亦會降臨。

母親，你可以復仇了。

You Are Cordially Invited...

The body of a young female was discovered in the basement of a long–abandoned, six story building on 12th street. Without any positive identification, the forensic team suggested she was 19 to 21 years old and without any obvious signs of trauma, they were unable to theorize a cause of death. She matched no missing person on record and by the level of decay, she had been dead for just short of a week. The only items found on the body were two pieces of paper in the back pocket of her jeans and a silver crucifix necklace lodged in her esophagus. The following is a transcription of the audio file reading, by the lead detective, of the two papers found on the body.

"Fuller: Detective Jason Fuller of the omitted police department. Case number omitted. November 5th, 1982. There's an address at the top of page one: 6117 12th Street. This location matches the address where the victim's body was found. Okay. (clears throat) Page one:

Welcome to Hell House.

Congratulations! A close friend has recommended you be invited to a very special Halloween treat! At Hell House, we are committed to providing a thoroughly immersive and terrifying haunted house experience. For the safety of you and our denizens, you must strictly read, understand and

地獄之家邀請函

位於第十二街一幢六層高的建築物裡，一個荒廢已久的地牢內，發現了一具年輕女屍。由於沒有任何身份證明文件，法醫小組估計死者年約 19 至 21 歲，而且沒有任何明顯的創傷跡象，他們無法判斷死因。她不是失蹤人口，而根據腐化的程度，她已經死了一個星期。唯一在身上發現的物品是她褲後袋的兩張紙和卡在其食道中的十字架銀項鏈。探長在死者身上發現了兩張紙並讀出了紙上內容，以下為錄音的文字版本。

「Fuller：本人是隸屬 XX 警局的探員 Jason Fuller。檔案編號 XXXX。1982 年 11 月 5 日。第一頁上方有個地址：第十二街，6117 號。位置與發現屍體的地址吻合。好的。（清喉嚨）第一頁：

歡迎來到地獄之家。

恭喜您！您的好友邀請了您來到這個非常特別的萬聖節盛會！在地獄之家，我們致力提供一個既全面又擬真的恐怖鬼屋體驗。為了您和我們居民的安全，您必須謹慎閱讀、理解並遵守以下條例。

follow the below guidelines.

1. Have fun! This is imperative.

2. Only guests 18–27 years of age are permitted inside Hell House.

3. Creatures and features of Hell House and its affiliates are not allowed direct, physical contact with any guest, under any circumstance. No exceptions.

4. A maximum of 2 guests are allowed inside Hell House at any time.

5. Weapons of any kind are not allowed on or within Hell House property. Including, but not limited to: knives, guns and fire.

If you understand the above requirements, you may now enter Hell House where further rules will be explained.

Fuller: turning to page two.

6. Implements of faith, such as crosses, bibles, holy water and prayers are aggressively forbidden on or within Hell House property. Failure to adhere to this rule will result in your

一）玩得開心點！這是必須的。

二）地獄之家只准 18 - 27 歲的客人入住。

三）在任何情況下，地獄之家及其附屬機構的生物和特效不得與任何客人有直接身體接觸，沒有例外。

四）任何時間都只可有最多兩位賓客進入地獄之家。

五）不得攜帶任何種類的武器進入地獄之家，包括但不限於：刀，槍和火。

如您了解上述要求，您現在可以進入地獄之家，稍後將會跟您解釋更多條例。

Fuller：翻去第二頁。

六）嚴禁攜帶任何信仰物品進入地獄之家，如十字架、聖經、聖水；或在地獄之家進行任何宗教儀式，如禱告。如觸犯此條例則會使您自動豁免條例三。

automatic exemption from rule 3.

7. If separated from your party, please use the emergency exits located in the basement and the 8th floor window. Our workers are here to help you.

8. The Doctor is real and is exempt, in perpetuity, from rule 3 and 5. Under no circumstance, are you to acknowledge the Doctor's presence lest you be held to fullest extent of rule 12.

9. If you experience any sudden pain, nausea, paralysis or explosive miscarriage during your visit to Hell House, seek the Doctor's attention immediately.

10. Rule 2 does not apply to virgins and guests that are with child.

11. The basement is strictly off limits to our guests.

12. To ensure authenticity, some scenes may depict loud noises, death, torture, personal fears incarnate, horrifying visions, and unauthorized third–party control.

13. Run. We like that.

Fuller: What the fuck?"

七）如跟同伴失散了，請使用位於地下室及八樓窗口的緊急出口，屆時將會有工作人員提供協助。

八）醫生是真實的，而且永遠不被條例三及條例五所限。在任何情況下，您必須承認醫生的存在，否則您將需謹守條例十二。

九）如果您在地獄之家遊玩時遇到任何突發性疼痛、噁心、癱瘓或爆發性流產，請立即諮詢醫生。

十）條例二不適用於仍是處子及與小孩同行的賓客。

十一）地下室屬禁區範圍，賓客請勿內進。

十二）為了確保真實性，某些場景可能會出現巨響、死亡、酷刑、反映個人恐懼、驚嚇畫面以及未經授權的第三方控制。

十三）跑吧，我們很喜歡的。

Fuller：這他媽的是甚麼啊？」

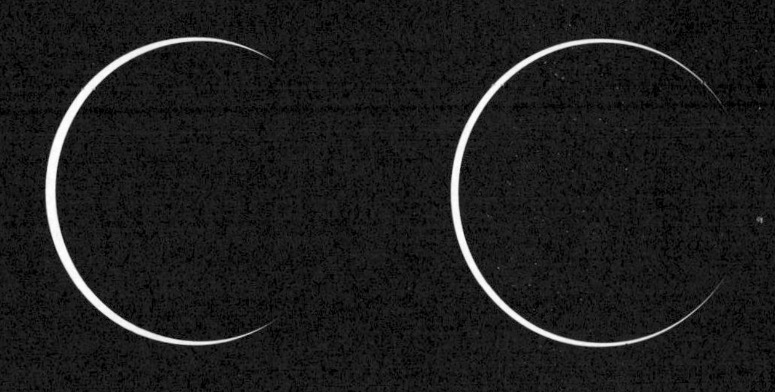

BOOK OF NO SLEEP　無眠書

編譯解讀

以下僅為個人理解，並不一定或完全代表作者原意。

詭譎童話

家人從來都不聽我講話 • 18

主角一出生就夭折了，而父母不知道他的靈魂一直依附在家中。

Sally 的宵禁 • 20

Sally 就是怪物，Bucherman 太太一直在保護主角和其他朋友。

童言無忌 • 22

Alison 一直都在說真話，只是沒有人相信她。

雞湯 • 23

主角為了趕走後母，不惜在自己的湯裡下漂白劑。

有個小孩走進我的店跟我說他爸爸死了 • 25

小孩沒有說謊，但父母都是他殺的。

圍欄後面 • 29

主角從小就被拐帶了。

肥豬 • 31

主角也把自己當成一頭真正的豬，自焚起來，衝向「象群」。

想像樂園 • 32

Sarah 不是個正常的小孩，甚至不是小孩。

Alice 的生日會 • 35

呼應愛麗絲夢遊仙境的故事，在現實或父母眼中，Alice 經歷的一切只是她的幻覺。

我床底下有怪物 • 38

住在主角樓下的小孩，一直都被他爸爸虐待。

我發現女兒把家貓淹死了 • 39

女兒在模仿爸爸殺掉 Jason 的過程來殺掉貓咪，而且爸爸回來後就會對主角下手。

惱人自白

我不再沒兒沒女 • 44

從 Jacob 出生那刻開始，主角就已經看上了他，最後更把 Sarah 殺掉了，把 Jacob 據為己有。

強迫症 • 46

主角將會殺了自己剩下的女兒，因為零也是雙數。

雙重謀殺的結局 • 47

乞丐是媽媽，小狗是兒子，而釘子就是丈夫施暴留下的傷痛。

鳥澡盆 • 49

主角正在因為當初曾對昆蟲做過的事而遭遇報應。

按「確認」以發送 • 50

公義已得到彰顯。

四十八正在等待 • 53

主角開始出現問題，他父母將以四十八取替他。

女孩互助互愛 • 55

主角幫助自己的方法就是把在酒吧認識的醉娃賣掉來賺錢。

心寒覺悟

末日啟示

生存規則

Contributing Authors
作 者

Atlani Godina

Brad VanHook

Brittany Miller

Claudia Winters

CommanderSection

Edwin Crowe

Gabriel Oro

James Marie Parker III

Jeremy C. North

Joseph Dean

Kyle Carag-Chiu

M.A. Santiago

Marie Mitchell

T. Ku

Morasyid

Tanja Simone

Nicholas Ong

V. R. Gregg

Noah Mester

William Roland-Batty

Raka Mukherjee

YKGem

Thank you for providing creative and breathtaking stories.
Thank you for making the book enjoyable and relatable.

BOOK OF NO SLEEP
無眠書

作者
Author
Short Scary Stories 版區作者
Short Scary Stories Authors

譯者
Translator
陳婉婷
Mia CHAN

特約編輯
Contributing Editor
羅慧詠
Venus LAW

印刷
Printer
CP Printing Limited

出版
Publisher
點子出版
Idea Publication

地址
Address
荃灣海盛路 11 號 One MidTown 13 樓 20 室
Unit 20, 13/F, One MidTown,
11 Hoi Shing Road, Tsuen Wan

查詢
Inquiry
info@idea-publication.com

發行
Distributor
泛華發行代理有限公司
Global China Circulation & Distribution Ltd.

地址
Address
將軍澳工業邨駿昌街 7 號 2 樓
2/F ,7 Chun Cheong St,
Tseung Kwan O Industrial Estate

查詢
Inquiry
gccd@singtaonewscorp.com

出版日期
Publication Date
2023-10-10（第八版）

國際書碼
ISBN
978-988-77957-7-3

定價
Fixed Price
HKD$98

點子出版
IDEA PUBLICATION

BOOK OF NO SLEEP

無眠書